Kara & Ty

For All those great

Memories together!

Love Dad +
& Mom B +

Sunset Beach
A History

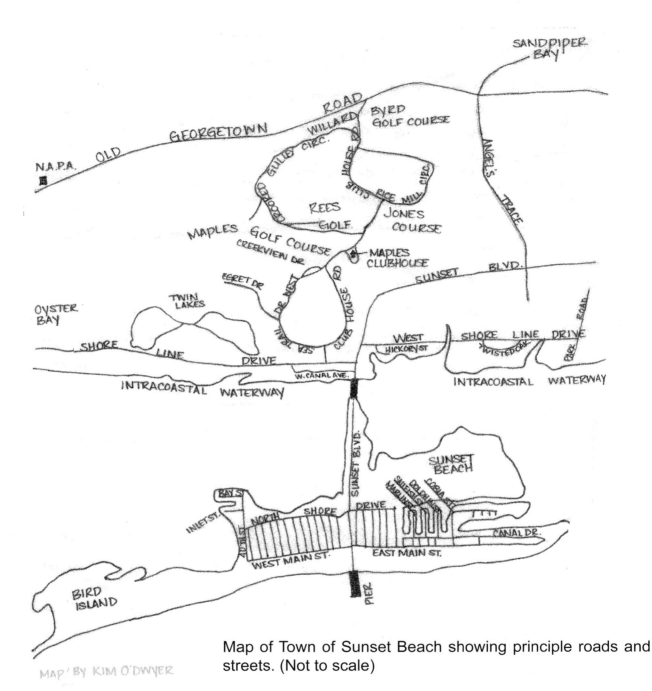

Map of Town of Sunset Beach showing principle roads and streets. (Not to scale)

MAP BY KIM O'DWYER

Sunset Beach: A History
© 2010 Jacqueline DeGroot
All Rights Reserved. No material in this book can be copied or reproduced
in any manner without the express written consent of the author. Excerpts for reviewing permitted.

Published by Silver Coast Press
Sunset Beach, NC 28468
www.jacquelinedegroot.com
www.millerpope.com

Cover and interior design: Miller Pope
Front and rear cover illustrations: Photos by Ken Buckner
Interior illustrations and photos by Miller Pope except where noted
Transcription: Pam McNeel
Editor: Kimberly O'Dwyer

Printed in Canada
ISBN 978-1-4507-2304-6

Sunset Beach
A History

Jaqueline De Groot & Miller Pope

4

A Tale of Five Centuries

Dedicated to Paul Edward Hughes

Ed Hughes was born in Pennsboro, West Virginia and until 1992, when he retired with his wife, Jody, to Sunset Beach he was employed by the Tower Hill School in Wilmington, Delaware where he served as Dean, Chairperson for the History Department, Principal of the Summer School, Coordinator of Special Programs, and Coach and Alumni Coordinator. His bio is quite impressive. With civic and church activities, it takes up three pages. It was fortunate for the town that in 1993 he took on the task of Town Historian. He gave lectures at various locations throughout the year so that newcomers could learn the history of the area, and he was working on a history of Sunset Beach when he died. Which is how I came to be sitting at my computer writing this dedication.

Shortly after Ed died in 2005, people began suggesting I finish the book he started. I knew him socially, so whenever we met, I would ask how far along he was on the book. He was noncommittal; I could never get him to tell me how close he was to having it completed. At the time he died I had no idea if his book needed a cursory edit, was a stack of pages in need of typing, or a collection of notes and newspaper clippings.

One day, a very persuasive Susan Seidel insisted I call Jody, who was packing to leave the area to live with family in Delaware. She said it would be horrible if all of Ed's hard work and the treasure that could be Sunset Beach's only history book was lost to us. The box containing Ed's work had recently been returned to Town Hall after a handful of women on the island reviewed it. This should have been my first hint. I later found out that they didn't know how to proceed with it and, due to family illnesses, none of them had the time to devote to it. I mustered up the courage to call Jody and was surprised at how enthusiastic she was about my working on the book. She was delighted that Ed's work could still become a history book of the area. I was both shocked and buoyed by her confidence in me. I arranged to go to Town Hall to pick up the box.

A few days later it was delivered into my hands without fanfare—a typical cardboard box, not heavy, not large, and closed by crisscrossed flaps. I was surprised no one wanted an accounting of the contents. But no one paid much attention as I opened it and delved inside. No notebooks. No computer discs. No floppies, printouts or files. No flash drive. However, there was a bulging folder with newspaper clippings and two hand-written pages with years noted in one column and events in another—one on vellum, the other, a continuation of the first, written on the back of an "Elect Paul (Ed) Hughes to the Sunset Beach City Council" flyer. My stomach dropped to my sandal-clad feet. There was no book. What had he been doing all those years when he was telling everyone he was working on it?

In the bottom of the box, in a single layer, I noticed a series of cassette tapes. One by one, I picked them up and noted the names written on the labels: Sam B. Somersett, Linda Fluegel, Vernie Hickman, A.O. King, Ronnie Holden, Ed Gore Jr., Clete Waldmiller, Ray & Carmel Zetts, Shelton Tucker, Mary Katherine Griffin, David Stanaland, Brian Dennis Griffith, Dean Walters, Nivan & Frances Milligan, Mason & Ginny Barber, Julia Thomas, Frank Nesmith, Cherry Cheek. All in all there were eighteen interviews. I knew I had discovered gold.

It took the better part of a year and a half to have the tapes professionally transcribed, and it was a thankless job for my friend Pam McNeel, who deserved much more than I was able to pay her. The quality of the tapes was horrible, the accents and voices hard to distinguish, and the settings where the tapes were made, while often bucolic or coastal were not conducive to audiotaping.

Finally, I was ready to start writing. Six months later I was overwhelmed with the project. There is so much more to producing a quality history book than the writing. I needed pictures, artwork, and someone who knew all about design, layout, and illustration. I asked my good friend Miller Pope to join me on this venture. He agreed.

Ken Buckner offered us the use of his wonderful photographs and we managed to beg and borrow many more. Our appreciation goes out to many. While only two people responded to our ads for information, each contact led to another and soon eighteen interviews became forty, and . . . the rest is history—*Sunset Beach: A History*.

We thank everyone who contributed local pictures: Denise Bordlemay, Pam Callihan, Sylvia Henderson, Dean Walters, Ed Gore Sr., Sam B. Somersett, Charlie & Aileen Smith, Alex Mearnes, Buzz Lambert, Miriam Marks, Dave Nelson, Ginny Lassiter, and Seaside United Methodist Church.

Thank you, Ed Hughes, for the many hours you spent tracking people down and then getting them to talk to you. Without your interviews this book would not have been written.

Jacqueline DeGroot and Miller Pope

Preface

We believe that the history of a town is about its people. It's easy to read through the records and see all that has been done, but it's not so easy to absorb the spirit, the courage and the vision until you delve into the hearts of those who came before us. And there are a lot of "us" these days who would like to know what Sunset Beach was like in its infancy.

Some parts of this book may seem redundant as we have endeavored to tell each person's story in their own voice, and of course many people had the same experiences and knew the same people as Sunset Beach was a small, intimate community—until the last decade.

Ed Hughes, a councilman and an avid historian, made eighteen cassette-recording tapes, which the profiles are based on. In the three years we've been working on this book, we've added a few more. I thank Jody, Ed's wife, for turning Ed's work over to me when he passed—they are pure gold. Some of the people he interviewed are no longer with us, so that makes the tapes priceless. We were hoping Jody could receive the first copy of this book, but she died in June of this year.

The profiles printed herein are hearsay—as I've only been a property owner since 1992, a resident since 1996—I wasn't around for much of this. Many statements have been corroborated by others and major events have been substantiated by research, but often, as is in the case of storytelling, the ones who live through the event get to color the tale. So with leeway, we give you . .

Sunset Beach—A History

Many thanks to all those who contributed their stories and photographs, especially Ken Buckner who gave us carte blanche with regard to his wonderful photos.

Thanks also go to Kimberly O'Dwyer who helped with research, writing, editing and proofreading.

Thank you to our proofers who had to give up many beautiful summer days so we could make our deadline: Marci Callen, Jean Dean, Peggy Grich, Kimberly O'Dwyer, and Sandy Spinatsch.

Jacqueline DeGroot and Miller Pope

About This Book

This book is not a chronicle of everyday town government minutiae. If you seek a record of town council battles and meetings you will have to seek it elsewhere.

Politics cannot be totally avoided in an honest history of the town so the authors have tried to present the opinions of the towns' citizens in their own words. They are not necessarily the opinions of the authors.

There is little debate that the number one issue that has fueled conflict among town factions for years has been "The Bridge." As this is being written, the war that has raged for decades and has cost the state and federal treasuries millions of dollars is at last over. The court has spoken—a new high-rise bridge will now serve the town.

The opening of the high-rise bridge that will connect the island of Sunset Beach to the mainland this September—and replace the charming one-lane bridge that has served the community for over fifty years—ends one of the longest running verbal, legal and financial debates in Sunset Beach history.

On one side of the debate has been The Sunset Beach Taxpayers Association, which represents an unknown number of people supported by several environmental groups opposing a new high-rise bridge over the Waterway. They wanted to preserve the quaint and unique old bridge and safeguard the quiet lifestyle of the island by stemming development.

The arguments for the new bridge have been public convenience as well as fire and safety issues. Both residents and visitors have been subjected to long waits to get over the old bridge. It has been disabled for days, stranding people on the island and fire trucks on the mainland. Also, the cost of repairing and maintaining the old bridge has been costly. With the issue of the bridge finally resolved, it will be interesting to see what conflict will raise the next furor. The installation of the sewer system is now in progress; pros and cons for legalizing terminal groins (submerged anti-erosion seawalls) are being debated back and forth; height limitations are continually being contested, and the town is trying to make improvements while being mindful of today's economy.

Over the years, there have been many issues that have caused division between the townsfolk, and almost all of the interviewees mentioned being involved in a passionate debate or two. Debates aside, the Sunset Beach residents interviewed recalled life as it was when the area was just coming into its own, when times were simpler, hard work was rewarded, and watching the sunset over the ocean was the best entertainment there was.

At the end of the day, after all is said and done . . . we are all blessed to be here, in this paradise by the sea. The people in this book have contributed to this endeavor by telling their stories. Without them this book would not have been written. And so . . . we give you a journey through the past,

Jacqueline DeGroot & Miller Pope

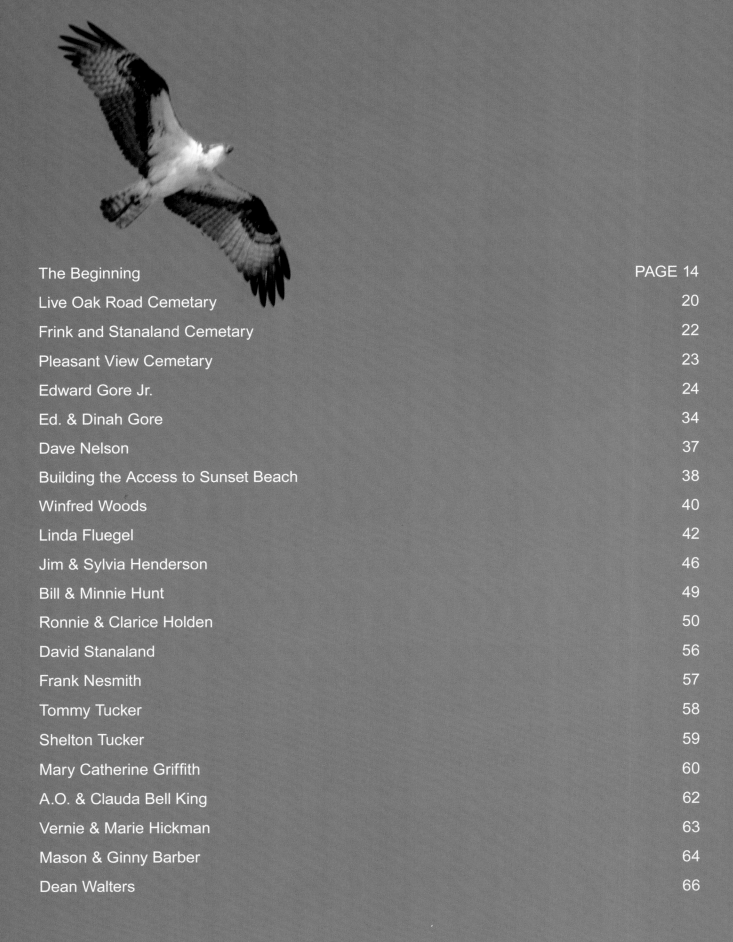

The Beginning

Sunset Beach as a separate island was born during Hazel, the great hurricane of 1954, the second worst storm since hurricanes acquired names. It struck almost exactly on a high tide and devastated the coast of Brunswick County, creating Mad Inlet and sundering Sunset Beach from Ocean Isle Beach.

Sunset Beach along with its sister island, Bird Island, is on the border between North and South Carolina and enjoys a very benign climate. It is the same latitude as Los Angeles, has the same average temperature, and is more southern than half of South Carolina. In addition, the island is unusual among Carolina barrier islands in that its beach is accreting sand instead of eroding.

What is today considered the mainland portion of the Town of Sunset Beach, is in fact, several islands joined together by bridges and causeways. When most people refer to "the island" they mean only the barrier island. Sunset Beach was not even an island until the Intracoastal Waterway was excavated in the mid 1930s.

Until very recently in geological history, Sunset Beach, along with the entire coastal plain of the country, was under the sea. Fossil evidence of this is not hard to find.

The first inhabitants were Indians, but it is believed that they only visited the island to dine on seafood. No evidence of any long-term habitation has ever been found.

The first European to visit the area was Giovanni da Verrazzano, exploring in the service of France. His exact landing site is unknown.

Until the 1720s, virtually the only people to visit the area were pirates and Indians. But soon, Europeans discovered that a profit could be made fishing, lumbering, raising rice and indigo, and tapping the pines for turpentine, pitch and tar, needed for the ships of that era. Naval stores were a big commodity in Brunswick County as every ship needed to be sealed against leaks and the ropes treated to prevent rotting.

Men from Brunswick Town helped eject Spanish invaders who had come to steal slaves from the area in 1748. These men also played a part in winning the American Revolution.

In 1791, the Gause Family hosted President George Washington at their plantation, three miles from present day Sunset Beach. Washington was traveling on the Old Post Road, which ran directly through the town. A section of the old road has been preserved as a cart path at Sea Trail Plantation.

The barrier islands of Sunset Beach and Bird Island slumbered through the decades with few visitors until they were awakened by the Civil War. Men of the area joined the Confederate Army and served the South making

salt by evaporating seawater. Salt was an essential because without it food could not be preserved and people as well as animals had to have it to survive.

The local population served the South by helping to unload beached blockade runners. When a blockade runner was intercepted and prevented from entering the Cape Fear River or one of the many neighboring inlets, it was forced to run up on the beach. The Confederates would hold off Union landing parties while the locals attempted to unload as much cargo as possible before blowing up the

ship. The metal hulk of the blockade runner, The *Vesta*, was set on fire in ten feet of water in January of 1864 and is now under the parking lot of the Sunset Beach Pier, once known as Vesta Pier.

The war ended and the island napped once again. Times were hard and most of the population lived a life of subsistence, barely surviving by farming, fishing and hunting. The barrier islands were considered practically useless, good only for grazing cattle. Sunset Beach was isolated from the rest of the county because the roads that existed were deep sandy ruts at best.

A hurricane around the turn of the century destroyed the rice dikes and the war left the planters with no money to repair them. The cultivation of indigo ended during the American Revolution with the loss of the British subsidy, and the decline of wooden ships lessened the demand for naval stores. Hence, the "Tarheel State" was no longer the world's leading producer of turpentine, tar and pitch. Times were hard for the local farmers. However,

the introduction of tobacco brought in some money.

Hard times continued through the Spanish-American War and First World War. The Great Depression made conditions even worse. Then came prohibition, and prosperity for some as the new law provided an easy way to make a profit.

The remoteness of the area around what is today Sunset Beach, with its many inlets and waterways, provided a near perfect layout for smuggling. Rumrunners were quick to seize the opportunity. It is said that the father of one of our country's presidents took advantage of the situation around Sunset Beach for his illicit booze importation business.

During the Second World War, Coast Guard sailors mounted on horseback, patrolled the beach for spies set ashore from Nazi U-boats.

A few years before WWII, two events occurred that began to open up the area to the world. One was the completion the U.S. Intracoastal Waterway and the other was U.S. Highway 17, the county's first paved road.

Land was still of little value except for hard scrabble subsistence farming, and land on the sandy barrier islands was considered almost worthless for anything except cattle. But change loomed on the horizon.

Said to be the oldest cemetery in Brunswick County, Live Oak Road Cemetery is on Seaside Landing Road at Seaside, right behind Walgreens. The cemetery dates back to the mid-1700s. Bricks are piled in a fashion similar to the way the early Indians buried their dead. However, since the bricks are believed to have come from the ballasts of ships, it has also been theorized that the bodies of early sailors, docked or settled at Seaside Landing at the end of the road, were carted inland and given a proper burial. As this was well over two hundred years ago, and there was no Intracoastal Waterway to hamper any makeshift cortege carrying both body and bricks a few miles inland, they might even have come from the area that is now the island of Sunset Beach.

A split rail fence erected by the first Sea Trail Homeowners Association, situated in the Seaside Station area, marks the area and pays homage to the first Sunset Beach residents to settle in the area—or so it's believed. There is little likelihood that they were slaves, but that is also a possibility. A stone bench allows visitors to sit and reflect, to imagine the time and place as it was long ago, and to ponder the identity and character of the people buried there.

Less than fifty yards from the number 8 building of the River Creek Condominiums in Sea Trail is the Frink and Stanaland Cemetery. William Frink, his wife Annie, and five of their children are buried there, as well S. Bunn Frink a local attorney and famous statesman in his day. It's been said that he did not have the most stellar reputation, but that if you were the one in trouble, you definitely wanted him on your side. The amount of his fee was rumored to depend on whether or not he was to provide the witnesses. He died in 1989 at the age of 90.

The Frinks owned a large plantation in Ocean Isle and we're told they treated their slaves like family. A slave traded or sold to the Frink Plantation was set for life. Descendants of these former slaves speak very highly of the Frinks. The reason there are so many Frinks in the area now is that it was a common practice for slaves to take the last name of the plantation owner they worked for, and all were proud to take on the name of Frink. People are still proud of the having the name today.

The Stanaland side of the cemetery has the most recent gravesites, most in the 1900s, a few into the 2000s. You can see how devastating typhoid fever, tuberculosis, and other childhood illnesses were in the late 1800s and early 1900s as there are quite a few gravesites honoring young children who succumbed to disease.

The cemetery is still in use. Every few years you see a vault being delivered, a canopy being erected, and chairs being situated around a gravesite. It's a rather odd view for the vacationer who looks off his deck to see the grandeur of the first hole of the Maples Golf Course competing with the bucolic dignity of a well-attended funeral.

The Pleasant View Cemetery, also known as the Frink/Long Cemetery, is located off Old Georgetown Road, just past the Planter's Ridge Entrance to Sea Trail. It is an old cemetery that is quickly being recaptured by the environment. Wooden stakes mark gravesites for locals who died in the 1800s, among them the Reverend Reuban Long and Samuel Frink. It is often referred to as The Old Slave Cemetery, so presumably slaves were buried there also.

Edward Gore, Jr.

For Edward Gore, Jr., first son of Ed and Dinah Gore, Sunset Beach would appear to have been the perfect place to grow up, a veritable playground with surf, sand and abundant tree frogs close at hand. But although interesting and educational, it was a tad lonely for a child born in 1960. It was not easy to root out friends in the days before the northern exodus and the advent of massive coastal development.

Edward Jr. was born at James Walker Hospital in Wilmington, NC, which was torn down in 1967 along with Community Hospital to make way for New Hanover Regional Medical Center. His father and grandfather were working on setting up the Twin Lakes Subdivision at the time. Access to the island of Sunset Beach had just been accomplished the year before—up until then you had to be a bird, have a boat, or swim amazingly well to reach the island.

The causeway was built up from the material brought up from dredging the creek that can be seen just to the right of the road when you are going over to the island. It has been called Gore's Ditch and Jink's Creek; on the Army Corps of Engineers maps it's referred to as Big Narrows.

The dredging boat was built by Mannon C. Gore, Edward's grandfather. At the time there was no money to buy that kind of machinery and it had to be customized for Mannon's purposes anyway.

Edward's grandparents lived in the house that became the Italian Fisherman Restaurant. It was right next to the Intracoastal, on a little bluff overlooking the island. Edward remembers playing in the big old oak trees on the bank, especially the one on the corner—the one tourists step out of their cars to photograph while waiting for the bridge. Artists from all over come to paint the quaint bridge with that same majestic tree in its foreground. He says he used to climb right on up into the center of it and go all the way to the top. Can you imagine the view? Looking out from that vantage point, a little boy could surely fire off his imagination. On a clear day, he could envision pirate ships coming over the horizon. This is a part of Edward's childhood we can all easily envy.

When Mannon built the original bridge in 1958, the top of that tree would have been a good platform for a spectator to watch the activity had there been any around. Alas, the tourists were all at Myrtle Beach or at Wrightsville Beach, not at Sunset Beach. Hence, the need for a bridge...to get everyone over to the ocean.

The young Mannon, having recently served in the United States Navy, had been an amazingly observant fellow while in many different ports. Despite having only a sixth grade education, he took away complex mechanical concepts and engineering principles solely from memory. Few, today, manage to master his grasp of hydraulics and machinery even after years of college. That he had a gift for common sense and engineering was a given. That he had a dream, just beginning to come to fruition, would soon be known to all.

According to Edward, the bridge is pretty much the same as it had been then. The floating part is different he says, but the oft-repaired deck looks the same as it did all those years ago. He adds that the state has replaced every piece of it since—at least once. The original bridge that Mannon built was the same style as the current bridge, although the encroachments were not as wide. If you were to crawl underneath the bridge at low tide, you'd notice the old stubs of the pilings from the original bridge. They were cut off at ground level, below the water line when the state put down the new pilings that are encased in concrete.

Young Mannon Gore

24

Edward remembers seeing the old pilings and asking his father why they were down there. He was told that the state rebuilt the bridge to their specifications when they took over the maintenance in 1961. There had to be so many houses per mile for the state to take over, so they must have just met the criteria. The bridge was rebuilt in 1973, again in 1984, and a few years ago the decking was replaced yet again.

Mannon not only designed and built the bridge, he was also the first bridgetender. Before the state took over the daily operations, he would leave the bridge in the open position for boat traffic and if anybody wanted to come off the island at night, they needed only to blink their high beams at his bedroom window for him to come out and close it. Few permanent residents lived on the island at that time so I doubt his night's sleep was disturbed all that often.

Mannon sold his development company at Sunset Beach to Ed and Dinah when he and his wife, Mina, divorced in 1970. The company operated out of a little office next to the main house beside Milligan Twin Lakes Grocery (built between 1957 and 1958). The grocery store later became Shark's Beachwear and is now the highly controversial Waves store. Edward remembers when the building that housed the development company was built in 1964, as it was one of his earliest memories. The grocery store was already there as it had been built in 1961.

There were no children on the island at the time, and just one family living on Shoreline Drive that had kids he could play with. The parents, Bill and Joanne Simmons, lived in a brick house, the second on the left as you leave the boulevard heading towards Calabash. It was an ice cream shop at one time but has since been torn down. The Simmons came to Sunset Beach from Whiteville in 1964. Bill Simmons was a schoolteacher and Joanne was a teacher's aide. They both taught at the little school in Shallotte that was moved a few years ago.

Edward attended that school until fourth grade before being transferred to Union Primary School when racial integration was implemented. Then he went to Lockwood Academy for two years before going to Shallotte Middle School for the 7th grade and part of 8th grade. Then it was on to Waccamaw Academy in Whiteville for the last half

of 8th, 9th and 10th grade before ending up at West Brunswick High School for 11th and 12th grade. You wouldn't think someone who grew up in such a small community would have attended so many schools. It sounds as if Ed Jr. was run all over the county. There just weren't enough schools or teachers back then.

A couple of families in Calabash, over on Thomasboro Road, formed a carpool for six to eight kids, including Linda Fluegel's daughter, Sharon. They were ferried back and forth in a Ford van. It was an hour each way for the Whiteville trip—and that makes for a very long day for everyone involved.

Bill and Joanne Simmons had three kids, two boys and a daughter. In 1970 they moved to Hickory for teaching positions so at the age of ten, Edward lost his only playmates.

He says he was very lonely because there wasn't anybody else to play with after they moved away. In 1972 there were 72 people who lived on the island of Sunset Beach, and none of them were children.

Most of the people living here were retired. Christine Brumetts taught school—she had actually taught Ed Jr. math in 4th grade at Lockwood Academy—her children were grown. The next kids to arrive on the scene were Ray and Janie King's kids. Their house sat in the right of way where the new bridge was built. They own King and King Builders.

For a while, Edward's "good aunt," the one who's from Tabor City, (called the "good aunt" because she never fought with anybody), lived here with her husband Robert, who worked on the dredge with Mannon. They lived in the little blue house at the end of the road across from the grocery store that was owned by Ed and Dinah and occasionally rented out. They had children, so Ed Jr. had cousins who were three to four years older than he was. But by the time he was old enough to be aware of them, they had moved back to Tabor City.

He vaguely remembers a couple of girls who lived in the house next to the house that the mayor and his wife used to own (the big white one that belonged to Monty Williams). Their father had been killed in a car accident when he ran into a pine tree on the big curve at what is now the east gate of Sea Trail. The tree was later removed by the North Carolina Department of Transportation. Edward can remember the night he was killed, but at that time he hadn't met the girls yet. One was his age or a year older, the other was two or three years older. She grew up and married Jerry McLamb over on Thomasboro Road. Jerry was a heavy construction contractor who built the course at Crow Creek and later became the superintendent of schools. Ed Jr. believes the family still owns a house on the Waterway.

Edward can't say he was the first child to ever live here, but he was the first and only one at the time the town was incorporated in 1963. David Kanoy was a young man when he moved here, but he can't remember when that was. The Kanoy's ended up buying the old house his parents had lived in that later became the office for Kanoy Realty.

Edward does not remember his grandmother on his father's side being around much except during the holidays. He says she was a stern woman and he figures that was because of the hard living at the time. It's a nice grandson indeed who can find excuses for his dour granny. He says that she never approved of Ed marrying Dinah. Some say it was because Dinah was from Beulaville in Duplin County. Back then families didn't always cotton to outsiders.

Despite his mother's disapproval, Ed married Dinah and they had three sons, Edward, Craig and Greg. Craig, the middle son, died when he was three and a half. Edward says his mother's family, the Eubanks, is as good as they get. He calls them the good-hearted side of the family. They never fight and get along well. His father's family, on the other hand, fight against each other all the time—except for that one aunt who he calls the decent or good one, who lives in Tabor City and is as good-hearted as she can be. His father Ed was a middle child, having two older sisters and two younger sisters. Dinah was one of nine siblings, with four brothers and sisters. Ed and Dinah's first

house was in the old Kanoy Realty Office, now behind Sunset Vacations. Before it was moved, the house used to sit on top of a hill on the right as you came onto the island. After a few years the family went to live on the mainland in a little brick house on the Waterway.

Edward remembers the house on the Waterway where two brass propellers used to sit, propped side-by-side (the house and the propellers are no longer there). He has fond memories of growing up there. With that view, who wouldn't? But at the time, there were only a dozen houses that were permanently occupied and there was no one to play with so he had to entertain himself. He had a dog and they would go walking through the woods exploring. That's pretty much all there was to do. And there were *plenty* of woods to explore—mostly all there was, was woods. It was unusual to see deer as they had a lot more habitat to live and hide in back then. But a few times he had a deer walk right past him, not twelve feet away. Foxes and raccoons were prevalent and occasionally someone would spot a bear. He almost stepped on a four-foot alligator one time when he was walking around one of the lakes at what is now Oyster Bay Golf Course.

Edward's parents, Ed and Dinah, having bought the development company from Ed's parents when they had split up, made payments back to them for many years after. Things were moving along, but everyone was still struggling to make the dream work. His grandmother stayed in the community while his grandfather, Mannon, moved to Florida.

Over the years, Mannon gave his daughters a legacy of land. He was generous in giving out lots to family members. Oceanfront lots that at the time sold for $8000—lots that are now worth ten times that amount.

The Gore family moved from the house on the Waterway to one on the beach in the early 70s. They had another house at the time which they tore down and then subdivided the acreage into lots for sale. Was this the first teardown? Hmmm . . . I wonder. The Gores were seriously starting to develop the island now and prosperity was finally in sight. What started out as a small enterprise, grew and grew, and is still growing today.

Mannon C. Gore

In the days before Sunset Beach, Mannon Gore had been a partner with Odell Williamson at Ocean Isle Beach. Both had visions, but they were being tugged in different directions. Things were beginning to change rapidly, in many arenas, too rapidly to keep friendships intact.

Then came the controversy about the inlet between Sunset Beach and Ocean Isle Beach—Tubbs Inlet. Edward says he remembers when they closed the inlet. When they pushed all the dirt into it and closed it up, he was ten-years old. There were two huge piles of sand that had been built up with bulldozers on the Sunset Beach side of the inlet channel. He says it looked like it was high tide. Only it couldn't have been because when they actually filled the inlet in, they wouldn't have been able to get the dirt ahead of the water fast enough.

He remembers the bulldozers pushing the dirt in and filling up that channel. They had taken the dredge and partly cut through a new inlet on the property line between his grandfather's property and the Sloan's property on Ocean Isle Beach. Because the inlet had moved westward, a big chunk of land that belonged to Mannon attached to Ocean Isle Beach and was inaccessible—he couldn't get to it.

I guess in Mannon's mind, the simplest thing to do was to move the inlet instead of moving his land. Back then you could do that, there were no laws against it. It wasn't that gigantic of an engineering project either, but Mannon made the mistake of cutting the inlet only partially through under pressure from the state. They were holding out, trying to get the state to come up with the funds to line that channel with rock so it could be permanently stabilized.

They almost succeeded when an unnamed fisherman dynamited it open the rest of the way.

They had to use leverage against the state to get them to come up with some stabilization. But, he says, it really didn't appear that they needed it. He adds that now there are an awful lot of rocks buried in the sand on the Sunset Beach side and there may even be some on the Ocean Isle Beach side. He's not sure.

Sloan sued Sunset Beach, Twin Lakes and Edward's grandfather. He doesn't know if his parents were named or not. That's the earliest lawsuit he can remember, and according to him, Sloan won because he had the best lawyer. He says that when you go to court, right doesn't necessarily win; it's who has the best attorneys or who puts on the best show for the judge or jury. He says, "It's all a show."

He remembers his father talking about how Rae Sloan, Tripp's mother, called him up after the trial and told him that they had no idea they'd been trying to get the state to stabilize the inlet. They weren't aware of that fact since it hadn't come out until the trial. She said they would have been in favor of that. Sad how these things happen.

When one thing goes wrong, others seem to follow. The Kanoys, originally from Charlotte, had been good friends with Mannon. They had built up a sizeable clientele, managing beach cottages on the island. They started out as the first rental agency, even taking over a few accounts for Mannon that he had dabbled in during the early 60s, as he no longer wanted to mess with that end of the business. The Kanoys built their business and had virtually no competition until 1972 when Jack Townsend opened Bay and Beach Realty, which soon became quite large.

Economics being what they are, expansion loomed and the islanders balked. Many did not like newcomers; it's still the same today. Once someone gets their piece of paradise, they start to resent the fact that anybody else with some extra pocket change can do the same thing and disturb their tranquility. It was the beginning of the islanders versus the developers.

The Kanoys, being loyal to their clients, had to side with the property owners and try to appease them for fear of losing them and their business. And of course, Ed Gore, who is all for promoting this as a Shangri-La for all to enjoy, managed to butt heads and tangle emotions. When Mrs. Kanoy became mayor, it's safe to say, there were some heated arguments on both sides.

Mannon started to build an arcade (not to be confused with the one that's on the corner now) where the gazebo parking lot is now, situated on what is now the extension of Sunset Boulevard, beside the old pier. Back then, the backside of the pier was a lot closer to the street because there wasn't all the sand that has since built up. The mayor got an injunction to stop the construction saying the arcade was being built in the street. According to Edward, the street was never actually a street. Mannon argued that the street was original plots of land that he owned and that had never been de-platted. They lost that battle when the town insisted that the main street went to the ocean. Of course, Ed Gore sided with his father and said Sunset Boulevard did not go to the ocean, that they had made a wrong decision. Who was the "They?" The beginning kernels of the Taxpayers Association. Battle after battle would ensue over the years as both built their clout. Financial ties made it politically expedient for Mayor Kanoy to take the position of her clients. Hey, business is business, and they were all struggling to survive.

In retaliation, Mannon and Ed put fence posts on some of their property so people couldn't trespass. The land where the gazebo is was one of the lots they fenced in. Shortly after, Ed, on a visit to the island, discovered that

Frank Nesmith had taken down some fence posts and had parked his car on the lot and was sitting on the fender taunting him. Edward says that when his father discovered that Frank Nesmith was purposely set up to provoke his father, Ed could not control his rage. He slashed all four tires and beat Frank up pretty good. It was the only time Edward has ever known his father to be violent despite acknowledging that he possesses a rare temper that can erupt from time to time. Ed Gore was hauled off to jail for that incident. But, as Edward states, "They were both at fault."

Soon 90% of the homes on the island were rented for the summer, and supply and demand being a major consideration, what with factoring in rental incomes—more houses went up. Kanoy Realty eventually merged with Bay and Beach Realty in the early 80s and relocated their offices across the street. When Mr. Kanoy became ill and Mrs. Kanoy could no longer run the business, she sold to, of all people, Ed Gore, Jr., who renamed it Sunset Vacations. Angst or no angst, money again was the issue. Ed Jr. says that, "People will ultimately look at their pocketbook no matter what the issue."

Mannon, with no ties, having split from his wife, decided to leave the town in his son's hands. He basically washed his hands and left the area. Initially, he went to Emerald Island for several years before settling in Florida. When asked about the divorce, Ed Jr. comically recalls that the reason might have been because of Mannon's drinking. He says he doesn't know if his grandfather had a drinking problem all long or if she drove him to it. He says he's heard mixed stories, but knowing her personality, he doesn't have a doubt that she had a hand in driving him to drink. He says, diplomatically, that she was a "negative person" while his grandfather was an optimist and didn't like people pouring cold water on his ideas. Mannon is remembered as a great guy and a decent whiskey drinker. In fact, he had a still right here on property now owned by Sea Trail. Mannon paid an old man a few hundred bucks to vacate his still and shed even though it was on property owned by him. He didn't want to deal with issues of squatter's rights and he wanted to make use of the man's still.

Even though Ed Gore has always had a proprietary interest in the town, his son, Edward Gore Jr., does not feel his father has ever run the town. He has managed to stay involved and was on the town council from day one until just a few years ago. No one can argue the fact that he knows more about the island than anyone and that he has a lot of foresight and knowledge in developmental issues, drainage, and infrastructure. But being a major landowner has always led to conflict of interest charges, which he adamantly denies. Being raised the way he was raised, watching his father's hard work as the island took shape, made him want to fulfill his father's dreams . . . to develop Sunset Beach and have it prosper.

And prosper it did. In 1976 four men got together and created a community that is still growing today. Sea Trail Plantation was once a part of the vast holdings of International Paper.

Tom Tucker, the broker in charge for Sunset Properties, whose father, Shelton Tucker, was the mayor at the time, was working with Sunset Realty, as it was called back then, as their primary salesperson. International Paper had contacted Mannon because he had bought the mainland property that formed the Twin Lakes Subdivision from them. Their real estate department in Atlanta had his number on file and called the office saying they had land in the area that they wanted to sell and was he interested?

At the time, the local businesses were having their own little recession and cash flow wasn't all it should have been. So even though they wanted to buy the property, they couldn't do it on their own. Ed Gore simply reached out to the people he had grown up with and asked if they wanted in. He put together a partnership to acquire the property because it had always been his father's dream to have the rest of the tracts as part of the town. Unfortunately, Mannon didn't live to see it happen. Edward says his grandfather would have been very pleased to see Sea Trail and to see how the town has grown to encompass the area all the way to Georgetown Road.

At the time the negotiations were going on, Edward had just received his driver's license. He was enlisted to drive his pickup to meet Tom Tucker in the Kmart parking lot on South College Road in Wilmington. They needed a particular document to close the deal as Tom Tucker was flying from Wilmington to handle the transaction. Ed Jr. was instrumental in the acquisition of the land now known as Seaside Station.

Ed Gore, Harris Thompson, Paul Dennis and Miller Pope became the founding partners. Ed knew Paul from church. They both attended Old Shallotte Church, out past Grissettown toward Longwood, where Mannon and his family originally hailed from. Harris Thompson brought in Miller Pope.

Harris and Paul were in the singlewide business and had started some mobile home developments toward Ocean Isle. It's what they knew and were comfortable with, but Ed had ideas for home sites and a golf course project that he eventually wanted to see come to pass. He finally got his way when they moved across the road, but just barely. Sugar Sands was initially scheduled to be mobile homes.

Edward fondly remembers that it was Paul Dennis who decided they could build individual homes. He was a hands-on kind of man and loved running a bulldozer and other heavy equipment. He was interested in building lakes, moving earth, making roads, ditches, and ponds. Everyone said he was very bright about doing things, much as Mannon had been, not a lot of formal schooling but an abundance of common sense. They could picture things in their minds and then figure out a way to do it and tinker and tinker until they got their ditch witches running.

When International Paper came back with another offer of land, Sea Trail was built up enough that it could acquire the large tract from them. It was about that same time that Larry Young was trying to build a golf course and he approached them about leasing Oyster Bay.

Ed wanted to build a golf course but the corporation did not. They knew nothing about golf, so didn't want to build a course. Larry Young built Oyster Bay, and Sea Trail leased the property to him with some very favorable terms. It was a wonderful deal for Oyster Bay and a defining point for Sea Trail. Without his example, things would have been very different for Sea Trail and the Town of Sunset Beach.

Sea Trail was glad to get the money for the lease as they had just spent a lot of money for the land. It was a no-brainer at the time but it's often said that they should have asked for more money. Of course everyone says that . . . except Larry Young.

Because of Larry Young, the Maples course came into being. The partners saw how much income he was generating and wanted some of the action. Ed was getting his wish, a golf course with home sites for people to build on. It's pretty much a given that, had Larry Young not come along with his proposal when he did, Sea Trail would have become one of the largest mobile home parks in the state.

But all was not bliss in this new partnership. Everyone came from a different background and with the death of Harris Thompson, new partners came into play. His two daughters and his son-in-law inherited his share. Harris and Dennis had many projects involving singlewides, so they understood that business; Miller Pope, a retired illustrator and owner of The Winds Resort on Ocean Isle Beach, had a creative mind and the ability to design; and Ed had the mind of a developer and businessman. But all too soon, Harriet Thompson and her sister Francis Williams, along with her husband John, had to be factored into the decision making process. Edward says that his father had always had a broader, bigger vision for Sea Trail than any of the other partners and, despite trying to enlighten them about the potential, they were rarely up to taking the risks involved. He succeeded in some areas and failed in others, and Ed Jr. says it's still the case today. It is probably the main reason they are all anxious to sell. They are not of a like mind and with each generation coming up and taking the reigns as directors, things get more and more complicated.

Developing Ocean Ridge was Ed Gore's way of showing that he knew what he was talking about all along. It has the original concepts he had envisioned for Sea Trail. But he had to have complete control to finally do it his way. Several years ago Ed gave Ocean Ridge to his sons, Edward and Greg to run and control. A few years later it was sold to Mark Saunders and his group.

After paving the way for so many people to build their retirement homes in both Sunset Beach and Ocean Isle, Ed and Dinah finally built their own dream house on the Waterway, just up from one of the houses Ed Jr. grew up in. They are very involved with the community, his alma mater, Campbell University, ballroom dancing, and supporting local charities.

Edward lives with his wife in a house in Sea Trail Plantation by Oyster Bay. He is into technology and communication systems. He owns Xaranda, a computer company providing Internet access and email and he also does trouble-shooting for his clients. He and his brother were partners in Sunset Realty and Sunset Vacations, but sold out in 1988. He bought the Century 21 franchise but doesn't see how to move forward with it at this time. He is trying to start a phone company but is being fought every inch of the way. His father can surely tell him that it's a feeling he ought to get used to.

Ed & Dinah Gore

Mannon Gore, Ed Gore Sr.'s father, was a native Brunswickian who grew up on Hale Swamp Road. The original family homestead was near Big Oak Supply. Mannon and Mina Gore taught Ed to cherish family, to work hard, to value integrity, and to be of service to others. Ed attributes these sacred principles to his parents, who were dedicated to their church and their family. He says they guided him with their ethical example.

After serving in the U.S. Navy, Mannon managed to acquire a thousand acres of land: 500 cultivated and 500 woodland. The land became the setting for his first house, which was a white bungalow on blocks at the end of Russtown Road. His farm was the last settlement on that road. With knowledge gleaned from his time overseas with the U.S. Navy, combined with ambition to prove himself and provide for his family, he struck out to make his fortune.

In 1953, he went into partnership with Odell Williamson and the two bought Ocean Isle Beach from its owners, paying just under $270,000. The joint venture floundered as both men were fiercely independent so they dissolved the partnership. 1954 Hurricane Hazel came to the coast and Mannon, seeing that Sunset Beach was unaffected by the storm, decided to buy and develop it. In 1955 he purchased the stretch of sand from the Brooks family, the largest property owners in the area. The development of Sunset Beach became his all-consuming passion. As that vision took wings, he was able to invest in other properties that eventually his son, Ed, would use to fulfill his own dreams.

In 1952, Ed graduated from Campbell University, then served four years in the United States Air Force. After his tour, which included the Soviet Union and Japan, he attended East Carolina University where he earned a business degree and learned Russian.

He met Dinah Eubanks, a native of Duplin County and former Miss Beulaville High, at Topsail Beach when she was living in Kinston. They married in 1959 and immediately joined Ed's father, the founder of Sunset Beach, in his coastal real estate development business. Both he and Dinah worked with Ed's father for many years, developing the island of Sunset Beach. In 1972, Ed and Dinah purchased the island and Twin Lakes, Inc. from Ed's parents when Mannon retired and moved to Florida. They became partners in Sea Trail Resort and Conference Center when it was started in the early 80s. Always hard workers with good business sense, they continued to prosper.

Ed has a great love of the area, recalling wonderful stories of the "old times," bringing history to life as he tells about the Cape Fear Indians, about finding arrowheads, pottery shards, and describing how they made salt. He recalls events with great detail, remembering names, places, exact footages, acreages, budgets, bids, and dates. He tells a story about Ralph Price, Bird Island, and Nivan Milliken, who was Mr. Price's caretaker.

Mr. Price wanted to build a family compound on 1,200 acres. So he built a bridge, the causeway, a caretaker's hut, and planned a house that he put out to bid. He had a budget of $250,000 (in 1960) for the main house. All the bids came in close to $350,000. On the heels of that disappointment, Mrs. Price was killed in a car accident.

Mannon, who got along great with Mr. Price and wanted to help out, had arranged for Mr. Harrelson of Middle Sound, in the Ogden area, to do some dredging for Mr. Price, as he himself didn't have the time. Then Mr. Price's son also died, and the compound that was supposed to be five houses plus the main house didn't seem worth the time and trouble anymore. Shortly thereafter, the wooden bridge, which Ed remembers as having creosote sides, caught fire. The wind was blowing out of the east that night, making the flames look like waves leaping in a storm. He says it was a spectacular sight. Many watched it burn. Some say the fire was started by someone who had a grudge against Nivan, who was known to be quite rude. Some say it was the fishermen who were not happy with the dredging and wanted access as there was no way to get around the bridge. Others say it was a love affair gone wrong—maybe a woman scorned, as the high dunes have always been a favorite place for trysting. A few say it was to keep the island from being developed; there was talk of a resort now. But all who were there that night acknowledge it was no accident. Everyone recalls the gasoline can that was left at the scene.

With his father, Ed and Dinah donated the land and loaned money for the first Town Hall to be built. Years later they took back the lot the old Town Hall had sat on and exchanged it for a larger lot. Over the years, the Gores have donated or sold property at reduced prices to the Town. In 1985, they donated valuable beachfront property for parking at the Gazebo.

In the early 90s, Ed and Dinah decided to go solo. They had learned that the frustrations of trying to persuade partners to a more refined way of thinking were counterproductive. They were dreaming big this time. Ed wanted to bring a truly premier community to the beach.

Mannon had acquired the Brooks' farm near Sea Village and that land, along with more added over the years, eventually came back to Ed. In the 90s, he and Dinah began developing the property as Ocean Ridge Plantation, an upscale golf community to rival anything on the coast. He knew there were buyers who wanted to live in an exclusive upper class community. It turned out he was right.

During the development process, disposal of the Somersett farmhouse came up and Sam B. Somersett was offered the house. Moving houses was a pretty common practice back then, but Sam didn't need the house and no one else in the family wanted to pay move it. Ed didn't want to see it demolished though, so it was moved and refurbished and can now be seen from Route 904. Ocean Ridge homeowners can tend garden plots around the farmhouse if they choose to. So many participate that the farmhouse has flowers blooming year'round; it's a quaint little farmhouse, well kept and alive with a bountiful harvest, just as it might have looked many years ago.

Ed sold Ocean Ridge Plantation to Mark Saunders in January of 2004 after he and Dinah made plans to phase out and hand off some of their business endeavors to their sons, Ed Jr. and Greg (another son, Gilbert Craig, died when he was a small child). They now enjoy philanthropic participation in many charitable and educational organizations, attending civic functions, and spending time with family and friends. Dinah has become a celebrity ballroom dancer, and Ed is a very active member of the Kiwanis, Lion, and Rotary Clubs. A couple that has always done what they could for the community, even in the early days when they didn't have that much themselves, they continue to enrich the lives of others.

Ed and Mannon Gore

In total, Ed has served the town for forty-two years, most of them as a town councilman. He also held an appointed seat on the Planning Board from 1974-1990. He and Dinah have played the role of ambassadors, serving the town's interests and representing the town with regulatory agencies and courts, donating time and money to projects the town has supported, including the bridge, the sewer system, fire and rescue teams, the police department, the medical center, the Planetarium, and many school, church, and community programs. Ed's alma mater, Campbell University, has greatly benefited from his and Dinah's generosity and he is a distinguished member on the Board of Trustees as well as a chairman of the Campbell University Foundation. Our own Brunswick Community College has also benefited from Ed and Dinah's generous donations and continued support. In fact, the Fitness and Aquatic Center is named after Dinah.

Those who knew Ed when he was growing up, working alongside his father and getting indoctrinated into the business world, all say he was one of the hardest working people they've ever met. Often working well past the dinner hour, he was the one who knew how to use tools, operate heavy equipment, and get his hands dirty. He showed up when there was a job "needin' doin'" and tackled it. Those who know Dinah say she's always been a giver and a helper, the first to respond when someone's in need.

For Ed and Dinah it hasn't always been easy. But the years of struggling have paid off; their family is one of the wealthiest and most respected in the county. They have created a wonderful place for so many to live while carrying out their own dreams and following Mannon's vision for Sunset Beach.

Dave Nelson

Dave Nelson started coming to Sunset Beach in 1965. As a kid he lived in Lenore, NC, the self-proclaimed Furniture Capital of the World. His father's friends, Randy and Vera McGowan, were vacationing in Myrtle Beach and saw a sign for land auctions. Ed Gore was selling lots on the island of Sunset Beach. His father's friends attended one of the auctions and bought a lot.

At the time, there were only ten to twelve houses on the island. J.C. Alred had just bought the house at 805 West Main Street for $13,500—brand new, oceanfront, and fully furnished. He began renting it to Dave's dad for $75 a week. For Dave, it was the beginning of a lifelong love affair.

The first time he came over the bridge, at the impressionable age of ten, he knew that someday he'd end up here. He says that his family loved it here so much that, "We lived 51 weeks for the 52nd," just so they could go on vacation.

He regrets now that when they got to the house that they pretty much stayed right there. Looking back on it, he would have liked meeting the locals and catching up with them over the years. But it was just too much fun being there, living right on the beach. They would get up at six in the morning, go to the pier for bait, and fish until it was suppertime, around seven or eight.

The house was between 34th and 35th Streets and he remembers there being a fishing hut nearby. The fish were so plentiful that people used nets so large and heavy they needed a tractor to drag them in.

Curious to meet more of the locals he missed talking to as a kid, Dave recalls stories his neighbors on the island have told him throughout the years. He tells the story of Jim Bowen from Wampee, NC, a Korean War Veteran. He was a Marine and one of "The Chosen Few" selected for an offensive against the Chinese. It was during the winter and the Chinese slaughtered them. The wounded men lay in the snow for three days pretending to be dead. Jim was one of them. Recuperating in Charleston, SC, men from his unit often visited him. In those days, a service man got paid only once a month and many times they collected money for him, which he gave to his wife, Jacquelyn.

She used the money to buy property from Ed Gore at a land auction. The lots were on the east end of the island, around 13th and Cobia Streets. When Jim was able to leave Charleston, they opened a campground for pop-up campers and pull-behinds. They even had a clubhouse for their guests. Jim, along with his wife and two daughters, who were teenagers at the time, ran the campground for several years before selling off the lots. Jim and his wife currently live in Black Mountain, NC where Jim is being treated at the Veteran's Hospital in Asheville.

Dave says that a lot of poker was played on Sunset Beach back then, and that Jim was a big poker player. So was Mannon Gore—and often, land changed hands.

Dave, one of the leading sales agents for Century 21 Sunset Realty, is lauded as a premier builder and developer. He also owns The Sunset Beach Inn on the island. He has certainly found a way to end up here.

Building the Access to Sunset Beach

Top left: the dredge
Top right: the rotating section of the bridge
Bottom left: pumping to make the road toward the island
Bottom right: the completed access

Winifred Woods

Winifred Woods was elected Mayor of Sunset Beach in 1969. She was a very popular mayor and it seems she was very well thought of by practically everyone. In fact, the first town hall was dedicated in her name. The soft-spoken, white-haired lady with the gentle English accent was 72 when she took over the helm, 74 when she gave it back.

A Northerner born of English parents and the widow of an officer of Chase National Bank, she moved to the South in 1950 and lived in the Sandhills area until 1960. When she found a pretty little white cottage at Sunset Beach, she bought it, despite thinking that she couldn't afford it.

She had been in Myrtle Beach traveling, as she was so apt to do, and was venturing far and wide when she discovered Sunset Beach by mistake. When the house caught her eye and she realized it was for sale, she inquired, saying to herself, "I can't possibly afford that place." She nonetheless bought it the next day.

Known as vibrant, attractive, and a woman to be reckoned with, people often mistook her as being fifteen years younger. She was definitely no little old lady, just ask Ronnie Holden.

Her political career dropped into her lap, unplanned and unwanted. A lady with a feisty nature she had shaken things up in the community, irritated a few people in the process, but accomplished what she set out to do—some took note and thought to put her to good use. She was appointed to an unexpired term on the town council, then elected to fill the seat in 1969. Shortly thereafter the council selected her as mayor when Mannon Gore moved away. When her term expired she was unanimously reelected. The mayor pro tem was also a woman after that election, Frances Kanoy.

Born in New York City, but promptly taken back to England where she was supposed to have been born, she lived there with her parents until the age of eight when her parents took her back to America—to Yonkers this time. Her father was a world traveler with multiple degrees from many universities and apparently no need to use any of them. He fascinated her and she absorbed what she says was ninety percent of her knowledge from him.

She married William Wood, the son of an old prominent family. She lived with him in his family home on Long Island until he died in 1949. A year later she moved to the South to see if she could earn a living. She worked in an office at a hospital in Pinehurst and, as a hobby, renovated and sold houses in the Sandhills area. She had no need for the money at that time, but a great need to feel worthwhile.

This was good training since the position of mayor she would eventually accept came without pay. In fact, she always overspent her $125 annual allowance for expenses by two to three hundred dollars, buying things needed for the town out of her own pocket.

Her main motivation for accepting the position was so that she could serve the town and do what she could to keep it an orderly and attractive developing area. Despite knowing nothing about politics, she saw things she could do and got involved.

She said administering a town with two distinct personalities was very challenging. On the one side you had the mainland residents, retired people for the most part, who wanted to live a quiet, restful life. Then there were the beach people and the beach itself that drew thousands of tourists during the noisy summer making it a hectic,

loud and boisterous place.

In an article for The News and Observer (October 1971) she is quoted as saying, "We are going to have water here (a municipal supply) definitely within five years." Noting that wells and cesspools do not exist in harmony on 50-foot beach lots. "We could possibly put off the sewage disposal for ten years if we pipe water in." I wonder what she would think about the fact that we have put it off for not ten years, but for forty!

Zoning ordinances were enacted during her tenure and the town got a new town hall built on land donated by the Gores, built with contributed materials and many volunteer labor hours. It pleased her when it was done, because she kept the town records in the studio in her garage and nothing could ever be found in a timely fashion.

She attributed her political success to the fact that she had no local strings and was not in business, so therefore she had nothing to gain. No one owed her and she owed no one. She had no wants, had no needs, and she had "no axes to grind."

Although a registered Republican, she always voted for the person running, not their party. The G.O.P. asked her to run for a seat on the Brunswick County Board of Commissioners, but she declined. Her daughter, Katie Cotton of Wilmington, a horticulturist, was credited with creating the landscaped and terraced gardens that graced the mayor's yard. But no, Winifred did it all herself, following lessons learned from a father who taught her to tend her own garden from the age of six. Fond of painting in oils and watercolors, she used her spare time for occupational therapy, doodling with paint, as some seniors are wont to do.

Her house, on a small bluff, faced the marsh from her screened porch. She could see the strand and the sea and the fishing fleets heading for Tubbs Inlet. The marsh, hidden inside the channel, made it appear as if the boats were cruising on land.

For her 74th birthday (in 1971), Winifred didn't have a party. Instead, she had a public meeting on local dredging issues. The fifty-odd people who came to query the visiting engineers sang the birthday song to her at the end of the meeting. Not much more is known about Winifred Woods. She lied about her age so often that no one really knows how old she was when she died. But the Grand Dame certainly left a lasting impression on all who knew her.

Linda Fluegel

Linda began working for the Town of Sunset Beach in April of 1974. She was hired to assist the Town Clerk and worked two and a half days a week. In July, the town clerk moved to Wilmington and Linda moved into the position.

The Town Hall measured 500 square feet and consisted of one room with a large table in the middle where the Council held its meetings. There were six councilmen and at the time, the council appointed the mayor. Years later a referendum was held and the town charter changed to allow for the election of the mayor. Citizens felt the mayor, with the voting privileges of a councilman, had too much power. Now the mayor only votes as a tiebreaker.

The town employees consisted of: Linda, as Town Clerk; Norman Grissett as Police Chief and motor grader operator, and three Hewitt cousins who picked up garbage with the town's truck and dumped it at the town's landfill. The landfill occupied an area in what is now Sea Trail Golf Resort. All the employees were part-timers and paid below minimum wage.

Norman was kept busy grading the dirt streets. The only paved streets were: Shoreline Drive West (also known as Black Drive or NC 179 Business); Sunset Boulevard (also known as Beach Drive or NC 179); the causeway to Main Street on the island, and Main Street. They were, and still are, owned by the North Carolina Department of Transportation. The only dirt streets that were developed on the mainland were: Hickory Avenue; Canal Avenue, and Lake Shore Drive. All the town streets on the island were dirt. Deer would graze at the Town Hall and walk up and down Shoreline Drive.

There was never any traffic. Once Linda had a flat tire and had to use the owner's manual to fix it because no one was around to help. She had finished changing the tire and was trying to get the jack down when Norman happened by and helped her. Of course he laughed at her because he had never seen anyone change a tire using an owner's manual.

The only developed areas on the mainland were Hickory Street and Canal Avenue. A few houses were on the Waterway on Shoreline Drive West and a few on Lake Shore Drive along the lakes. The remaining areas were wooded.

On her days off, Linda would take her daughter and the town's old Royal metal typewriter to the beach. While her daughter played in the sand, Linda typed property cards. While she was typing she would think to herself, *Why does everyone go all the way to Florida? We have the same beautiful water, sand, and scenery right here.* "We would not see anyone all day. Once in a while we would see someone far off in the distance and they looked like they were an inch tall." Needless to say, in a few years people did find Sunset Beach and all the other Brunswick County beaches.

There were approximately 300 individual pieces of property. The rest were still in large tracts owned by Mannon Gore. When tax season came around Linda would drive to Southport, which was Brunswick County's government seat back then. In the early 80s the residents of Brunswick County voted to move the seat to Bolivia. It took her three days to get all the tax values for the properties for the town. All the tax records for Brunswick County were kept in large books, and done by hand. She would research the books and extract the information on each property in town. Then she would return to town and type the tax notices and record them in a ledger, mail them, and collect the taxes due. At this time, the town operated on only the tax money that came in. For a few years, the salaries of the town employees were not paid until the taxes had been collected. The town employees worked for three years without a raise.

As the island began to develop, the town hired a building inspector and the Town Hall was open every day except for Wednesday. In Brunswick County, in the 70s and early 80s, most businesses did not open on Wednesdays.

In December of 1979 the town provided public water to the island. In January, the mainland received public water. Norman drove Linda around town and stopped at each meter. She would jump out and record the meter numbers for each lot. She made up meter reading routes that are still being used today. At that time, the town had 300 customers. Linda manually calculated each bill, typed the invoices, mailed them, and then recorded the amount of money collected each month for each property.

In the 80s, a group of developers purchased a large tract of land from the International Paper Company. The Town Planning Board zoned the tract for mobile home development. The company became Sea Trail Corporation. It began with a community of mobile home lots called Seaside Station at Sea Trail.

During this time, the Sea Trail owners were asked by a golf course developer to consider leasing a large tract of their property to him so he could develop a golf course. A 40-year lease agreement was signed and Larry Young created Oyster Bay Golf Course. When the Sea Trail group saw that Mr. Young had a six-month waiting list for golf tee times, they turned their attention toward developing a community that would allow for golf as well as single-family homes. They brought their idea to the Sunset Beach Planning Board and an amendment was made to the zoning regulations to allow for such a development. Thus Sea Trail Golf Resort was born. It came within a hair's breadth of being developed with mobile homes.

Once the Seaside Station at Sea Trail subdivision was laid out, the developers petitioned the town to annex it. A great deal of effort was expended to keep this from happening. People were told that if the annexation was allowed everyone would have mobile homes in their backyards. The truth was, the majority of voters lived on the

island and they were afraid that if this subdivision developed, they would no longer have the majority vote.

As Sea Trail Resort grew, the developers petitioned the town for annexation of another section. Sure enough, once the area began to sell, the majority of voters did come from the mainland. The island residents have not had control of the Council since.

As the town grew so did its tax base. The town employees began to receive good raises and additional employees were hired. The town had many growth issues. Once the police force was established with three full-time officers, it was necessary for 24-hour coverage. The town still could not afford this, so the off-duty sheriff deputies filled in on an hourly basis. The police station was located in the town's work shop.

Garbage which previously had been dumped in a landfill on Sea Trail property, now had to be taken to the landfill in Supply since Sea Trail was being developed. With the town continuing to grow through annexation, more time was required to run it so everyone became full-time. In 1985 Larry Crim was hired to work full-time reading water meters and making sure the roads were graded. By this time Norman retired and, only a year and a half into his retirement, he passed away.

Billing water payments was now being farmed off to a professional billing company out of Charlotte. The taxes for Brunswick County were coded by town so Linda did not have to research every parcel to check if it was in Sunset Beach.

Around 1989, the town merged the Sunset Beach Volunteer Fire Department into the Town and hired a fire chief and two firemen. Sunset Beach was growing fast.

Linda reviewed building plans to make sure they met the zoning restrictions. She helped property owners and their builders with their permits. When necessary, she went out and did building inspections.

She became the first permitting agent for the division of Coastal Area Management Authority (C.A.M.A.), which allowed her to issue the C.A.M.A. permits and do the inspections for the town rather than the state having to do it. She had been a C.A.M.A. agent for over twenty-eight years when she retired.

Around 1987 the Town Hall was renovated. A 200-square foot addition became the police department and an additional 100-square feet was added for the Town Clerk's office and the computer room.

As the town grew, the staff grew and there was a demand for even more space. In 1994 the town swapped the land where the old Town Hall was on Shoreline Drive West for a larger tract on Sunset Boulevard and a new Town Hall was built. In 2005 the Town Hall was renovated and a police station was added. A new fire station was built at the same time, in the same place where the old stationhouse had been. For a while, the fire trucks were kept on the planetarium's parking lot so they would remain in a central area for call outs. And the town . . . well it just keeps on growing!

Linda retired in 2005 after thirty years of service to the town.

Jim & Sylvia Henderson

Jim and Sylvia Henderson, originally from Greenville SC, moved to Lumberton, NC, where Jim was in manufacturing. His company made Army clothes and products for Hang Ten.

They started coming to the beach in 1967 and Sylvia remembers walking the beach while she was pregnant with their first child, at the age of 42. They didn't like renting a beach house, so Jim decided to have a house built for them. They bought land on the west end, by the bay (across from the parking area at 40th Street). A.O. King built their first house and also the one next to it several years later.

One Expensive Bicycle was originally theirs. It was a small blue house on one level, with a gazebo at the end of the walkway. It was called *Another World* when they owned it because at the time, it was the last house on the beach where it connected to the bay. Only one-story houses were allowed then so a widow's walk was built on the roof so Sylvia could get up high enough to see the ocean. Window units were used for air conditioning, if there was any air conditioning at all. She recalls the power going out as a fairly common thing, and several times they lost everything in their fully stocked side-by-side refrigerator/freezer including the seafood they had caught. No one had generators back then.

Sylvia remembers that they used to baptize people in the bay on Sundays. She watched the community grow during their frequent vacations to the beach. Eventually, she and the children joined Jim during the summers as he had started building houses at the beach. Jim Henderson built many of the houses on the island.

The Hendersons became good friends with Mannon Gore who, Sylvia says, got the short end of the stick when he and Odell Williamson parted company. She says that, "Mannon was a real charmer." They moved from Lumberton to Sunset Beach at the height of the first building boom and Jim ended up building twenty houses on the island. He also built the Sunset Grocery, now known as the Island Market. She says her husband owned it for a while and rented it out to Don Porter. Then, when he sold it to Jim Milligan, Tommy Tucker ran it. Tommy was the mayor's son.

Jim and Al Odom had a business partnership until about the time Mannon left for Florida, so they were frequently on hand for some of Mannon and Bruce Kannoy's, "developer issues." Their office was upstairs in the grocery store, so they were in the thick of things. She recalls that Kannoy's office building was actually owned by Jim at one time.

Sylvia remembers Mr. Price, a wealthy insurance man who came from Greensboro. He owned the island now referred to as Bird Island. He was going to build a road and install power poles because the family wanted to build a hotel at the western end of the island, but their bridge burned down as they were putting in a road to get there and it changed all that. Mr. Price's son was killed in a plane accident so that, together with the bridge burning, changed their plans for the hotel.

When it came to deciding on things, it did not go smoothly back then. She says they could not get together on the gazebo project with Bruce Kannoy, even though they had the material on hand to build it. And, that as soon as the idea for a new bridge was brought to the table, "Save our Bridge" T-shirts became the rage.

For the longest time, the land next to theirs would not perk so they had no neighbors. The last house on the west end, now known as *Sunset at Sunset*, is there now. For years they worked on filling in that lot. Al Odom finally managed to sell it to a doctor after it had been filled in enough that it would perk. "Now it even has a pool!"

she says.

She remembers the days fondly. Days when they would stop at Mannon's brother's produce stand on Highway 17 and have fresh vegetables with fresh seafood for dinner, then sit outside to enjoy the ocean breeze. She says she remembers an odd assortment of things such as: Mannon giving his brother a brand new Chevrolet Bel-Air; David, her son, who is now in his forties, playing with his sister, Laurie, who rode horses on the beach, and the ache in her heart when Jim sold the beach house on the ocean and built one in the interior of the island.

Jim and Sylvia moved to Charlotte and he has since passed away, but Sylvia still has one or two lots and the beach house on 37th Street that the family uses during the season. She comes to Sunset several times a year to enjoy the beach, visit friends, and to check out the new restaurants.

Another World (1973) known as *One Expensive Bicycle* (2010) is shown above.
Today it is the center house below.

The picture above shows Sylvia Henderson the first owner of what is now *One Expensive Bicycle* sitting on her oceanfront deck in 1973. The bottom picture shows the view today.

Bill & Minnie Hunt

A history of Sunset Beach would not be complete without mentioning the Hunts. Although some people feel they impeded progress, quite a few feel that they did not. The Hunts were instrumental in keeping the island quaint— the serene and uncluttered oasis that it is today. They were stewards who cared deeply for the wildlife, both marine and terrestrial. They enjoyed the camaraderie of friends and neighbors and, over the years, often hosted events geared toward keeping people in touch with each other.

It would have been wonderful to have the Hunt's perspective of history and to hear firsthand why they devoted so much time and energy to serve a community that often didn't appreciate their efforts, but Bill Hunt passed away a few years ago and Minnie declined to be interviewed. I regret not being able to talk to them about the passion they had, which left a legacy that we all share today.

I never met either Bill or Minnie. I saw Minnie at a Town Hall meeting at Sea Trail on January 23, 2002, but never spoke to her, and a few times after that I saw her in the grocery store. I knew of Minnie's trademark hats and of vitriolic arguments with those who challenged her, and I knew of her legal attempts to checkmate the town in the 27-year game of chess that was played over the issue of the new bridge. Regardless of your stance, you had to admire her gumption, drive, and intelligence. Whether ill-advised or not, she and the Sunset Beach Taxpayers Association thwarted town, county, and state governments with legal gambits carried out with military precision. We're talking almost *thirty* years here. That's devotion to a cause and a willingness to work hard for it. Whether you agree with her or not, few would be that dedicated to such an unpopular stance.

One day, maybe I'll get to talk to Minnie, but for now, everyone who visits the island owes the Hunts a bit of gratitude for being the stewards that they were, and for taking care of this magnificent paradise until we could get here. Other than the issue of the bridge, they did a lot of good—championing the environment and making sure everyone knew how fragile the ecosystem is on the coast. Minnie was passionate about other issues, but the bridge overshadowed them all.

Some say she was adamant against change; that she didn't want the island and her way of life to be affected by development, that she didn't want to share the island. I first came to the island in 1989, so I saw a different Sunset Beach from the one she first saw. I fell in love with it the way it was then, in the late 80s. We all fall in love with "our" island from our own unique vantage point—in the continuum of time that destiny deems we be introduced to it. Minnie must have fallen in love with the island the way it was when she first came upon it, in the 70s—a more intimate, more pristine—and definitely a quieter, gentler place. She would consider me an outsider; I came many years after she made her wondrous discovery. I love her island, but in a different way, my own way. I envy her the time she had here when the island was unspoiled and nascent.

Minnie and Bill owned an oceanfront house that they built on Main Street on the east end of the island. They were offered more money than was prudent to refuse for the just the lot, so they sold and moved the house to North Shore Drive on the west side, close to 38th Street. She no longer lives on the island permanently but comes back to visit from time to time. She was at her beach house when I managed to track her down on Memorial Weekend (May 28, 2010) and she declined an interview saying, "What I know about Sunset Beach is mine." She seems to want to be left alone with her memories.

Ronnie & Clarice Holden

Ronnie Holden has deep ties to Brunswick County; he has one grandfather from the Stanaland side and one from the Holden side. His grandfather, Benjamin Holden, was granted land on the Shallotte River in the 1750s. The Stanalands, who could neither read nor write, eventually changed their name to Stanley in the 1800s. Ronnie was born in Southport and raised at Shallotte Point. He says Shallotte Point was a quaint place back in those days. He talks about the fishing boats and the dances Mr. Gordon used to have at his Anchor Inn, by the old Hughes Marina (the Inlet View Restaurant is there now). Mr. Gordon also ran the Bon Jon charter boat, a very familiar sight on the water back then. Ronnie's father was in the U.S. Navy, serving in the Pacific during World War II, but retired to Shallotte and became a commercial fisherman dealing in shrimp and clams. Fishing is one of the things his family has passed down from generation to generation. Ronnie's grandfather owned Brick Landing Fishery where the old ferry was located at Ocean Isle Beach. Ronnie also loves the water and fishing.

Ronnie moved from Shallotte Point to Sunset Beach in 1970 with his wife, Clarice, a year after they were married. They were both young, only eighteen years old, but they decided to make a life for themselves here. Shortly after they settled in, Ronnie and Clarice opened Twin Lakes Seafood Restaurant at the Sunset Beach Bridge. Mannon Gore had constructed the building used for the restaurant in 1959, although it was much smaller than the restaurant we know today. He allowed Ronnie to rent it for fifty dollars a month for January, February, and March, with the agreement that they would buy the building from him after that.

Clarice was familiar with the restaurant business as her family owned Coleman's Seafood Restaurant in Calabash. Ronnie describes their decision to open a restaurant: "My wife, she was really raised in a restaurant. Her family owned one back home, and she taught me. She ran things, I did what she told me to do, and I still do." He adds that there were not a lot of businesses in the area at the time, including restaurants. With the exception of Bill's Seafood, built in the 1960s by Sam Somersett, there was no other place to get seafood in town. They found a niche and went for it. Ronnie would go out on a little skiff at night to the creek next to the bridge off the Intracoastal Waterway and catch fish and shrimp. They served what they caught the next day in the restaurant. Ronnie recalls, "The first year we moved here, we sat here. We were open from 11 to 9 and, for three days, we had no customers." Twin Lakes started as a small operation with Ronnie cooking everything and his wife waiting tables, but soon the restaurant became a fixture at Sunset Beach. The location itself draws customers. With a view of the Sunset Beach Bridge, the Intracoastal Waterway, and the island beyond, Twin Lakes is known for its views perhaps even more than its food.

Once Ronnie moved to Sunset Beach it wasn't long before he became infamous in the town. He tells a funny story about his move to the area, "When I first came here I didn't know anything. I'd just got married and Daddy had some land on the river, so I brought that mobile home and put it here (behind Twin Lakes)." Ronnie hired J.P. Russ & Sons to move the mobile home behind his restaurant. It wasn't long before Mayor Woods, a woman whose voice Ronnie describes as "so nice," because of her soft British accent, had something to say about that. He says he'd never even

heard the word zoning. She told him mobile homes
weren't allowed in Sunset Beach due to zoning laws. To
which he responded, "I bought this land I can do what I want with
it." And she said, "No, that's not the way it works."

The town council held meetings at his restaurant—there was no town hall at
the time so they paid him fifteen dollars a meeting to use his restaurant. They came to a decision about
his property and ruled he was not allowed to keep his mobile home there. A few months later, Ronnie purchased
a nineteen-foot sign for his restaurant. Mayor Woods paid him another visit and told him zoning laws prohibited signs
that tall. "So in 1973, she approached me and asked me to run for town council and 'see if we can't teach you a thing or
two about zoning.'"

Ronnie spent three years on the town council before the Sea Trail debates started and he decided all the arguing
just wasn't for him. He served three years on the town council with some of the big players in Sunset Beach politics:
L.D. "Tate" Benton, who worked for the county in mosquito control and who had a fish house where The Colony is
now located, Jim "The Colonel" Gordon, Ed Gore—Mayor Pro Tem, and Mayor Shelton Tucker.

The years following
Ronnie's move to Sunset Beach proved
eventful. When Ronnie and Clarice first settled here there were only four families living on the beach: Jim
Gordon and his family, Joe and Leola Spivey, the Kanoy family, and Jim Bowen and his son, who had a local campground.
Ronnie recalls that his brother, along with Nivan Milligan and Dale Leonard, built the first house on the beach in 1959
and that they had to use a generator for the power tools. He recalls that in the early 70s a tugboat hit the Oak Island
Bridge and destroyed it. The bridge that was at Sunset Beach went to Oak Island, and Sunset got a new bridge. That
was the last of the sentimental "old wooden barge."

Ronnie has good memories of Sunset Beach before it was commercialized: he reminisces about the shrimp boats
that fished out of Shallotte Point; he remembers when the Sunset Bridge was just a floating wooden barge and had to
be sent to Wilmington for repairs for two weeks every March—a cold time of the year to make the trip to and from the
island by boat; and he can remember Nivan Milligan's father, Warren, and the store he owned where his brothers used
to trade eggs for drinks and cookies.

But his most prominent memories involve the Gore family. "Mannon was still running things when I came down
here. He was a character but he was always very nice to me, so was Ed. He (Ed) always had oil or grease on him. He was
a hard worker." Mannon stayed in the Sunset Beach area for about four or five years when Ronnie was living at Sunset.
He describes Ed's father as "more lanky" than Ed. He can still recall Mannon's take on electricity, "This place (Twin
Lakes) didn't have any air conditioning and I was having it put in, and Mannon said, 'What in the world you putting
air conditionin' in for? Just open the windows and the breeze flows right through here.' Mannon grew up in a different
time, a time without air conditioning or even electric lights."

Ronnie has known Ed all his life. The Gore's house was across from Twin Lakes and in '74 or '75 they moved out
and Ed's sister, Barbara, and Eric Hunn turned it into a restaurant called The Bridgeside. They leased it to Don Porter
who ran it, and later it became the Italian Fisherman.

You couldn't escape the Gore family or the gossip that followed them. Ronnie remembers hearing stories from
his grandparents about Hurricane Hazel—the horrendous storm that split what was then called Bird's Shoals,
the area encompassing Sunset Beach, Bird Island, and Ocean Isle. In its wake it left Sunset Beach in two parts,

creating Bird Island and an unstable inlet between Ocean Isle and Sunset.

The storm that destroyed all sixty houses on Ocean Isle and killed eleven people also ripped apart the partnership of Odell Williamson and Mannon Gore. After Hazel departed, it was time to rebuild and Mannon had pretty much lost everything he had in the storm. Mannon and Odell weren't getting along very well at this point and, instead of rebuilding together, they decided they'd divvy up and go their separate ways. But Mannon discovered he couldn't get a loan from the bank because Odell controlled the bank. He couldn't pass on this opportunity, even without bank funding, so Mannon sold his farm on the mainland and bought Sunset Beach. Although Ronnie wasn't around when the storm happened he's heard the story more times than he can count.

Ronnie, like all the residents of Sunset Beach, grew up surrounded by gossip and rumors about the Gore family—he adds he can't substantiate the rumor that Bruce Kanoy and Ed Gore shot at each other, although it's a story commonly associated with the history of Sunset Beach. Whether it's rumors about land deals or the night the bridge to Bird Island burned and the notorious gas can was found at the scene, Ronnie has tried to mind his own business and concentrate on his family's instead. However, some stories are just too . . . interesting to ignore.

Ronnie says that one of Sunset's biggest unsolved mysteries happened in 1970, the same year he moved to the beach. The story about the night the Bird Island Bridge burned has been told different ways by many people, but they are uncannily similar. Ronnie gives his account of the incident: "Mannon had built a bridge to the island (Bird Island) for Mr. Price. Mannon wanted to take his barge to do some dredging at Mad Inlet. The Gores have always wanted to stabilize Tubbs and Mad Inlet. Mr. Price wouldn't let him go by the bridge. The bridge was a stationary bridge; it couldn't allow water traffic to go through. The dredge sank at Little River Inlet. They were rebuilding it when I came here. Two weeks later the bridge burned." Ronnie added, "I can't tell you one thing had to do with another." However, when it's mentioned that according to Nivan Milligan a gas can was found by the burned out bridge, he chuckles and says, "I think it might have been diesel fuel." The events of that night are still a mystery to the residents of Sunset Beach.

Another event that caught Ronnie's attention soon after he moved to Sunset was the night Tubbs inlet blew up. He remembers his mobile home shook that night. He explains, "Some say the fisherman did it because they wanted it open. Others said it was a very bad storm that night everything came through. Some people say Mannon did it. The Sloanes—who owned the property—sued the Gores. They won the suit for land that had been lost (rumored to be six acres). The east end of the island here was in two parts, which was two big sand dunes and because that blew open, it was possible sand built these up, then they leveled it out and put the whole east end of the island there.

"It was like Twin Lakes, that were just creeks to begin with. Look at all the land you get. You could do things like that back then—nobody thought anything of it. Shoreline here came through the dining room. I filled this much in here. When Marsh Harbor was being dug out, right here in Calabash, they gave away that dirt there. I hired a dump truck and got a couple of front loaders full out of it. I did it until they stopped me. A C.A.M.A. (Coastal Area Management Authority) man came and told me I couldn't do it anymore. I tried to explain to him, it's my land . . .

"Even that land where the fish house was, over by Oyster Bay, that's been filled in, filled in almost to the road. Mr. Benton did it himself. He used to be in business a long time ago with W. J. McLamb's father, Willie Joe. W. J. has Mac Construction. He has some equipment and he filled it in back then."

In 1985, Ronnie's wife grew tired of the restaurant business and decided she needed a change of pace. Ronnie bought land around the corner from Twin Lakes and built a series of small shops. Clarice opened her own shop, Island Breeze—an upscale clothing boutique. Ronnie adds, "I built those shops in '85. At the time she was working with me, but she wanted to do something else, and she was always interested in clothing." While he misses his wife's help at the restaurant he doesn't mind that she's off doing her own thing. "With her over there, it's like I'm on vacation, I don't have to do anything. When she comes back over here, she cracks the whip." He jokes, "I try not to let her come over because she wants to take over again." With its bright colors and vivacious fashions, Island Breeze has become a success, drawing women from miles around and tourists from all over the world.

The Holdens eventually left the mobile home and ventured over to the island. After eight or nine years there, they left their home on 3rd Street at Sunset Beach and moved to Ocean Isle. Ronnie wanted a house on the water, as a fishing enthusiast, he really wanted a boat. He tried a bit of golf too, but says, "Never could get good at it, so I just quit." Eventually Ronnie gave up on boats and became interested in flying planes with his son, Eric. Unfortunately, Ronnie hasn't been able to do much fishing or flying in a while. In 2000, Ronnie was hit by a drunk driver. He was in a coma for a month and had eight surgeries. His neck was broken in two places and his leg in fifteen. The doctors did not think he would live and told Clarice to prepare for the worst. But God had plans for Ronnie. He was out of commission for a while, but has since healed completely. In fact, he convalesced in a high-rise condo at Ocean Isle Beach as guests of Odell and Virginia Williamson. He used to fly jet prop airplanes with their son, DeCarol, and thinks, "Miss Virginia is the nicest woman he ever met in his life."

One of his most cherished possessions is a picture on the wall in his restaurant. It is a picture of Jack Lucas, the youngest man since the Civil War to win the Congressional Medal of Honor. Lying to join the Marines at the age of 14, he was six days past his 17th birthday when he used his body to shield three Marines from two grenades in a foxhole on Iwo Jima. He had 250 pieces of shrapnel in his body, in every major organ, but he survived to tell about it. He was a great fan of Twin Lakes Restaurant and came by once a year to see Ronnie, later emailing him weekly. On June 5, 2008 he died at the age of 80 from leukemia. He found a good and caring friend in Ronnie.

Nowadays, Ronnie and Clarice spend their time running their labors of love, his restaurant and her boutique, as well as chairing a slew of charity events and fundraising for Brunswick Community College, Communities in Schools, Widow's Mite, Angel Tree, and just about any charity involving Brunswick County. They could not be happier, he says, "I've been here so long and I really just love the people here." The young married couple who came to Sunset Beach has done well for themselves, they've got it all: family, delicious seafood, amazing clothes, good works for the soul, and the beach.

Despite being fairly open and easy to talk to, there is one question Ronnie avoids at all costs—how does he feel about the new bridge? He answers, "I'm not gonna take sides, because either way it affects my business." If the bridge breaks or there's a long line of traffic that doesn't move, people can't get to his restaurant—a big destination for tourists in the area. But he will miss the quaint bridge that's been just outside his door for forty years. He disagrees with Minnie

Hunt's attempts to stop the bridge over the years, saying fondly, "She's a character, that's all I'm going to say. I didn't agree with what's she's done," adding that he knew Bill Hunt and his first wife better. "I've got mixed emotions about it (the bridge). It's like watching your mother-in-law drive off a cliff in your brand new Cadillac."

David Stanaland

David Stanaland's family was one of the first families to inhabit the Brunswick County area. At one time his great grandfather, Samuel Bell, and his grandfather, Tobias Bell, owned most of the land in the Ocean Isle, Sunset Beach, and Calabash areas. Tobias inherited the land from his uncle who died from tuberculosis in 1905. Tobias and his wife looked after his dying uncle in his last days. In return he was left 1,226 acres of land that stretched all the way into South Carolina. The inherited land had a $3,000 mortgage on it, which Tobias was unable to pay. David's oldest brother, Ernest, gave Tobias the money but forced him to sign the land over to him.

Ernest became involved with a church and decided to deed the land to his eight siblings. Ernest kept his share, which was in the Ash area. In 1956 David helped his brother draw up lines to divide the property. Ernest's wife tried to claim temporary insanity on his behalf so she could keep all of the land. David ended up with land in the Ash area. He currently resides on Little River Road, on about 200 acres. Two large farms surround his house. He has also leased some of the land to relatives who live on the property. David picked this plot of land when they were dividing the estate because it is the area where he and his siblings were born—he actually lives in the same house. He reminisces about the house he lived in as a child, "I remember the old home because of my father, he went up to Rocky Mount, he had a job at the cotton mill. I remember my sister Mabel bringing Joy, my other sister and myself back here in about 1922 or '23. I vaguely remember the old house that way. No plumbing, no lights."

When the property was divided, some of his brothers and sisters decided to sell their shares. Others, like David and Ernest, preferred to hang onto theirs, "They say real wealth is in the land," says David. One of the fifty-acre tracts his family once owned is now valued at about $3,000,000 and the property closer to the coastline is even more valuable.

David didn't see a lot of the development of the area because he was in the military. He came back to Brunswick County after WWII and stayed out of the military for eleven years before he went back in 1957. David retired from the military in March of 1973 to live in Brunswick County full-time.

Although David doesn't have a lot of stories about the growth of his hometown, he does remember what it was like before there was any sort of development. David used to roam Sunset Beach when it was what locals called Bald Beach. He says that if you wanted to go over to the island, you had to go across at low tide on a riding mule or a horse.

David now spends his time cataloguing the records he kept over the years—he has tons of maps and deeds tracking the history of the area. His daughter, Julia Stanaland Wethington, helps him find information to document his family's history. David has some interesting relatives: his Uncle Walter took the fall for a whiskey pit Joe Kennedy had put in Brunswick County during prohibition. His uncle spent eight months in the Atlanta penitentiary and his Aunt Alice received a check from Joe Kennedy. With stories like these, we hope he gets his memoirs written down. David adds, "I have a good memory and the records that go with them, too."

Frank Nesmith

Frank Nesmith was one of the few who came to this town before it even resembled a town. Frank built his first house in Sunset Beach in 1958, with his father and his brother. It was a vacation home where they could enjoy the beach and take their boat out on the water. When they started building their house, the bridge had just been completed and there were only four houses on the island.

Frank has had several interesting run-ins with the Gore family during his time at Sunset, the first of which was before they had even built their house on the island. Mannon Gore was building the bridge and one night, and while it was still under construction, a barge came and knocked part of his bridge down and broke some of the pilings. Mannon managed to salvage a few of the pilings, which he then sold to Frank to use to help him finish building his home.

Frank moved down to the beach permanently in 1975. Other than a few more houses it was not much different from his earlier days here. "There just wasn't much going on," he says of the still-empty town. Frank joined the Taxpayers Association, as most early residents did, although his interests weren't very political. He adds, "I have seen a lot of controversy, and I decided a long time ago to try to stay out of it as best I can." Instead, Frank devoted his time to studying the geography and the history of the beach.

One of Frank's prized possessions are aerial photographs of the island dating back as far as 1949—before Hurricane Hazel, a hurricane that altered the geography of the beach drastically. He went to Washington D.C. and dug through the archives to find old maps and photos of Sunset Beach, cataloguing its history. He can give a complete history lesson on the inlets and how the storms and construction have changed the area. He can also tell stories about the history of North and South Carolina from the early 1900s. One story in particular concerns property lines and how Napoleon Bonaparte Morris lost his land holdings, which included the South Carolina portion of Bird Island and oceanfront property, due to tax evasion. The holdings were then sold for $17, including recording and legal fees. Frank has donated countless documents and photographs memorializing the town's history to the Ocean Isle Museum.

Frank's days in Sunset Beach weren't always so innocent. He got into quite a few spats with the Gores throughout the years. One in particular even resulted in a fistfight. Frank parked his car on property that, although unclaimed at the time, belonged to the Gore family. Frank and Ed Gore got into it and Ed punched holes in all the tires of Frank's car. The police were called. The Gores were able to produce a land deed and Frank had to pay a $25 fine for trespassing. Ed was charged with assault and had to buy a new set of tires. Ed received a two-year suspension. Frank jokes that Ed got "Two years suspended upon the promise that he wouldn't beat me up for two more years."

While Frank no longer holds a grudge against Ed or the rest of the Gore family, he refuses to get into any arguments about the new bridge. He says, "I don't even discuss it with my friends." Frank feels it's time to change the bridge, a sentiment opposite that of most of the longtime residents of Sunset Beach. He says one defining moment changed his mind about the impending high-rise bridge. This happened while he was out on his boat. "There was a man on a jet ski with his young daughter riding in front of him and the cable was up and a boat was coming. I knew he was gonna make a turn and go through the bridge while it was open, but while it was being closed the cable was out of the water on that side of the Waterway. The guy came flying through there." Frank was able to stop the jet skier in time and tell him about the cable he would have hit if he'd gone through. "Chances are his daughter would have saved his life but she would have died. After that, I said, 'You know, the old bridge is picturesque and it gives the town a lot of class, but a high-rise would be safer.'"

There is no way to list all the things that Frank has done to protect the environment and to serve the town. He was instrumental in keeping development from spoiling Bird Island and worked to secure it for the State by giving tours and educating beachgoers on how fragile the ecosystem is on the coast. Only recently has he taken credit for installing the Kindred Spirit Mailbox, almost thirty years ago. He and Claudia, his girlfriend at the time, a free spirit according to Ginny Lassiter, came up with the idea and Claudia used to help collect the notebooks until she moved away.

Without Frank there would be no Bird Island. It would most likely be called Bird Island Resort-Marina-Spa-Casino-Yacht Club. We owe him a debt of gratitude and a prayer of thanks every time we walk those silver sands.

Tommy Tucker

Tommy lives at Key Colony on Marathon Island in the Florida Keys, he was happy to be interviewed by phone. The fact that he is no longer local may be the reason he was candid with his stories and observations. He is the son of Shelton Tucker, a former Sunset Beach mayor. He remembers when the Kanoys ran the pier, the height of the building boom, and the events in between.

Tommy moved to Raleigh in 1975. He worked in banking before moving back to Sunset Beach to work for Ed Gore, Sr. as a land broker in his real estate office. He worked for Ed for about four years. He bought the island grocery store from Don Porter, and Don Safrit ran it for him for fifteen years. Then he opened his own realty company, Sunset Properties, which he sold to Ron and Adrienne Watts in 2003.

He remembers the early days and says that Mannon Gore was an incredible visionary—capable and willing to do whatever he had to do. He says that Mannon and Ed were hardworking people; that they worked from 5:30 in the morning to dark, seven days a week. "They had property they had to sell and they had no one to fall back on but themselves. Mannon could be a 'rounder' and because of it, he and Ed split poorly."

Of Ed, he says, "Ed's a decent guy. Ed, in a crowd, was a fun person to be around," adding that, "Ed worked me just like a slave though—but we all worked hard."

He remembers the infamous fight between Ed and Frank Nesmith: "Frank baited Ed. And let me tell you, eccentric would be a kind word to describe Frank. I had just bought that store and in comes Frank. He was wearing a white suit. He says, 'Tell your buddy I just took his fence down.' I said, 'Frank, what the hell are you thinkin'?' I tried to get him to go put it back up. 'Nope. Nope. I want you to call him.' So I called Ed. Ed came over to the island and saw what Frank had done to his fence. Frank had a pale blue Pontiac. Ed pulls out his pocketknife and flattens all four tires. Then Ed hit him straight out. Frank's arms flailed like a scarecrow. He made no effort to save himself. Mr. Gugen was Frank Nesmith's attorney and Ed's was Mason Anderson. The Judge was Wilton Hunt, who later went to prison on drug charges. I was one of the few witnesses. Ed claimed trespassing and Frank claimed assault. Ed got a slap on the wrist."

Tommy also remembers Norman Grissett, the first policeman. "His ultimate demise was when he started drinking on the job. He got fired when he drove the town motor grader into the marsh. Policemen did it all back then, as times were tough. Norman's literacy was just enough for him to sign his paycheck; he couldn't write a ticket."

He asked me if I knew about Bill's Seafood and how it got its name. I didn't, so he enlightened me. "Joe Peed took it over from Ivey. Joe was not a North Carolina resident so he got his brother to sign the liquor license—his name was Bill. People called him Bill for thirty years even though he wore a T-shirt that said 'Joe.'"

And speaking of T-shirts . . . Tommy says that Bruce and Francis Kanoy and Bill and Minnie Hunt were the primary anti-bridge proponents. They had *Save the Bridge* T-shirts that they wanted him to sell in his store. He told them, "We've been friends for twenty-five years. You don't want the bridge, but I do. I sat them down and talked to them so we could continue to be friends."

He says it was definitely commercial fishermen who dynamited Tubbs Inlet and then rattled off a long list of locals who were arrested for running drugs in the 70s and 80s, saying it was a big epidemic—and a fiercely competitive business.

He has nothing but admiration for Miss Rae, Debbie and Tripp Sloane (of Ocean Isle Beach), saying that they are all hard workers. He remembers Rae Sloane driving the garbage truck when no one else was available. Sometimes the police chief did too. "And Ed," he says as he laughs, "I remember him getting out of his Cadillac on a Sunday morning in his suit, holding a pipe together while a worker fixed it."

He chuckles and says he knows of two separate incidents when local adolescent males and their passengers did the Dukes-of-Hazard dive with their trucks, plunging into the Intracoastal because they tried to beat the bridge. Once in the mid-70s, and once just a few years ago (everyone managed to make it to shore, a broken arm being the worst casualty).

Tommy has interesting observations about the people he knew way back when. He reminisces about Art Rotundo, Jim Gordon known as the Colonel, the Kanoys, Bill and Minnie, Frank, Ed and Mannon…"People would rather climb a tree to hate each other than have a picnic on the ground. It was highly political, highly charged."

What he has to say about northerners…"If it wasn't for A/C, northerners wouldn't be here." And about the good old days at Sunset Beach…"Despite everything it was a nice community; then the Miller Lights would take over—and like a Cuban family, they'd fight like hellcats among themselves—but nobody better insult them outside their circle."

Shelton & Marie Tucker

Shelton Tucker discovered this area at a time when most people would have chalked it up as a loss. Hurricane Hazel had just wreaked havoc on both Ocean Isle and Sunset Beach, but Shelton saw something most people didn't—beauty and opportunity. When he moved to Sunset, Shelton became very involved in the community; he probably knew more about the goings-on in this town than the original founders. Shelton served as mayor of Sunset Beach for several years, although he can't remember whether or not he was elected by board members. Shelton was mayor when the town went through some major changes and had hit its peak for development. He has been a first-hand witness to the town's growth, watching it emerge from a town devastated by Hurricane Hazel to a prospering, thriving community.

Shelton and his wife, Marie, drove down the coast after Hurricane Hazel in 1954. As they made their way back they stopped at a number of islands, taking in all the devastation. They stopped in both Ocean Isle Beach and Sunset Beach. Access was not available to the islands so they waited for a cable ferry. When they got to the island they saw three houses that had survived the storm. Shelton recalls that day, "I don't think it was on that particular day, but shortly after that, we came back and we purchased a lot on Ocean Isle Beach. The first house that I built was on Ocean Isle." Shelton purchased a lot from Tripp Sloane, Sr. at the old pier location and began building in 1961. The Tuckers lived in the house on Ocean Isle Beach in the off-season and rented it during the season, until 1969 when they moved down permanently. After they became acquainted with Ed and Mannon Gore, they moved to Sunset Beach.

Shelton had been in the U.S. Air Corps during WWII and then "tried out" the insurance business until 1974. There wasn't much opportunity in the area for anything but building and development, so Shelton hopped on the building bandwagon. "After I got down here it was a matter of finding something that I could fit into in the area, and quite frankly, down in this area the main thing was development. So I would buy lots and build houses and basically, I would build to sell. That was it. It was at the appropriate time, we were never big. In other words, we were always small with what we did." His son, Tommy, says his father built maybe six houses, just dabbling in the construction business. It was very informal, it started during the course of looking around. Shelton became acquainted with Mannon and ended up buying one whole block from him, five lots between 10th and 11th Streets. The first house he built was on 11th Street and East Main Street in 1968. Tommy remembers that renters caught it on fire in 1974.

Shelton got to know most of the people in the area through his construction business or through his time as mayor. He says he used to know just about everybody in Sunset Beach, but it wasn't long before he couldn't keep up with the influx of people.

The Tuckers lived in an oceanfront house on Sunset Beach for many years, but in 1988 they moved to the mainland. He describes the reason for the move, "The reason that I built it and came over here was my wife had medical problems. Even at that point, and I felt—she didn't complain about it—but I felt that if by any chance I failed to get to the mainland due to the bridge, that would be a bad deal for her." Shelton missed the island life and continued to go over there regularly for many years. His son, Tommy, had an office on the island, so Shelton would often pop in and say a quick hello.

Marie passed away in 2003 and Shelton, at 93, lives at The Champions in Porter's Neck, north of Wilmington. According to Tommy, his father has many girlfriends and still drives. Tommy, still beach-bound, lives at Key Colony on Marathon Island, in the Florida Keys.

Mary Katherine Griffith

Mary Katherine Griffith moved to Sunset Beach in December of 1972, although her family has always lived in the area. The Sellers side of her family hails from Shallotte Point. She is also related to the Milligans, so she has a lot of "kin" in the area. She can remember when Hurricane Hazel came in 1954, her grandparents lived in Shallotte and there were only two shared telephone lines—it took nearly a week to get word that they were alright. Mary Katherine has seen this town change drastically over the years that she and her family have lived in Brunswick County. She says that when she moved to the Twin Lakes area where she lives, they still set out steel traps. She often worried when her dog didn't come home for days at a time. Fortunately, he was never hurt.

Mary Katherine didn't intentionally move to Sunset Beach. When she graduated from college, Brunswick County was the only place that was hiring and she had a job offer here. Her immediate family lived in Wilmington, so she commuted every day for the first year and a half. Then she rented half of a duplex from Shelton Tucker on Ocean Isle Beach. The year after, she moved to a cottage on Canal Drive. Mary Katherine loved living on the water but when her mother died the following year, she bought a lot on the mainland and built her own home.

Mary Katherine's political career began soon after she moved to Sunset Beach. She, along with a group of property owners, was instrumental in keeping mobile homes out of the area that would eventually become Sea Trail. They believed the property would be worth more if it were developed with stick-built houses instead. They were right. The

owners of Sea Trail decided to scratch the mobile home idea and develop the area as more of a high-end resort. Time has proven that this was a very good decision.

Because of her community involvement, Mary Katherine was launched into the political arena. She was on the Planning Board for a year and a half and on the Town Council for thirteen years. During her years in office, Mary Katherine made many friends, and of course, inevitably, a few enemies. It was unavoidable as she was at the forefront of several big issues including: the Food Lion Annex; the bridge negotiations; the sewer debate, and concerns regarding the development of the area.

Although Mary Katherine and her family have been here for decades, she fought the good battle to be accepted by the headstrong locals who wanted to keep the area restricted. Throughout history, people have always struggled to keep their *Shangri-La* to themselves and Mary Katherine understands that. She says, "It's like they want you to come in and buy the land, but they still felt like it's their land." Development was inevitable, so Mary Katherine tried to make sure that the area expanded gradually, and that places that had come to mean so much to so many didn't get lost in the process.

She will tell you that, if you go back far enough, everybody in this town is related. She adds, "One of my cousins and I have done some research on the family history and sure enough, Milligans, Sellers, Holdens, all of them are in the family background—it's quite interesting. You find Milligan spelled different ways in the county but we're all from the same roots." She says her great uncle, Beamon Sellers, helped Mannon Gore with the first bridge. He was working in Wilmington with the Army Corps of Engineers at the time.

Mary Katherine has seen this area emerge from a place where her great grandparents had no indoor plumbing to a town bursting with potential. She looks at all the new development in the area and stands in awe, "It is amazing to see how far this county has come."

A.O. & Clauda Bell King

In 1968 A.O. King saw potential in Sunset Beach, so he purchased the first property on Sunset Beach that he intended to build on and turn for a profit. At the time there were about forty houses on the island and development was on the verge of a boom. A.O. (A.O. stands for Alfred Owen but he never uses either name) was from Tabor City where he made his living in the tobacco business. He was also in the warehouse business in Hickory but, when he sold his part of the business, he decided to invest in property down by the water. He had purchased another piece of land in 1963 on Shoreline Drive, but hadn't done anything with it. A.O. moved down to the coast permanently in 1976 and began building houses in the area. He says of his foray into the construction business, "I had done a little building for Daddy growing up, my daddy was in the saw mill business and he built some, too. He taught me how—might not have been too good. When I first came down here I bought these lots and I decided I was going to build either one or two for speculation in the summer. And I got to building like that. Then the first thing you know, we were building them for other people."

The spec houses A.O. built launched him into a construction whirlwind. Over the next five years, A.O. built 230 houses on the island. He says he had good timing when he moved here, things were starting to explode, building-wise. He says you could buy any of the lots on the island for about a thousand dollars; the first house he built cost only $8,500—and it's still standing. When he first moved to Sunset Beach, the Kanoys were the only people who lived on the island permanently. They ran the pier as well as a realty company. He got to know what he calls "the somewhat reclusive" family pretty well in his years of building on the island.

Brunswick County was a very different place when A.O. first moved here. He recalls the local restaurant, Coleman's, once owned by Clarice Holden's parents: "They had the first restaurant in Calabash. First time I ever went down to that restaurant a long time ago, they had wood floors and long picnic tables. You walked in and sat down, they set the food on the table and you'd eat all you wanted for seventy-five cents!" He remembers only one restaurant and a country store being in the town at the time.

But A.O. is glad to see the area expanding and getting bigger. He says, "I knew that was going to happen, we all knew that. Question was how long? Nobody had any idea this place would ever develop as fast as it did. From '61 to '68 it didn't do anything."

Unlike several of the locals who moved to the island early on, A.O. decided town government was not for him. His son Greg, who moved down in 1955, did serve on the town council for a few years. A.O.'s reasons for not getting involved were simple: he didn't want to get in the middle of the ongoing battles between his friends Ed Gore and the Kanoys. He adds, "Oh yeah, they always complained. When I first came down here there were two factions down here: the Gore side and the Kanoy side. I never did hear Ed complain about the Kanoys, but the Kanoys always complained about Ed." A.O. says he admires Ed Gore for what he's done for the town and his business. He says one of the biggest reasons a lot of people don't like Ed Gore is because he runs his business like a business and he's been successful at it. A.O. has lived in Sunset Beach for a long time. He helped build it up to be what it is now, and all he wants for the future is for it to remain a place for families.

Vernie & Marie Hickman

Vernie Hickman grew up in Brunswick County, by Hickman's Crossroads—named for his family's store located there. He experienced this area when things were much simpler, long before there were shopping centers and high rises. Instead there were fisheries and plenty of vacant land. The Sunset Beach Vernie knew was much different from today. Back then there were only four houses on his street, and his dad's store ran on the credit he provided—he also bartered with customers who wanted eggs or coffee. Vernie says he knew Sunset Beach and Ocean Isle Beach before they were anything.

Vernie started working for his father's store when he was just a youngster. He spent a happy childhood in the Longwood area of Brunswick County fishing and exploring the plentiful woods, even hunting squirrel and deer. He worked for the Atlantic Coastline Railroad in Wilmington until WWII broke out. Then he moved to the Washington, D.C. area where he worked for the Northline Ship Building Company. He toughed it out in the city for nineteen years, fighting the traffic and the crowds, because he knew he would be coming back to his childhood home—if he lived long enough. He met his wife, a Yankee from New York, at a square dance in Washington. He describes their meeting and courtship simply, "Her family had just moved down and she was a stranger in the area. We decided to get married and so we did." They had a son and two daughters, who would all eventually follow their father back to Brunswick County. After a long career he left the city. He recalls, "The day I left Washington, D.C. was the happiest day of my life."

Vernie moved back to Brunswick County in 1969. He bought a lot on the water from Ed Gore for $2,500. To this day, he still gets teased by his brother for having paid too much. Vernie started working as a building inspector and then got a job with the fire department—a job that left him plenty of time to fish. As soon as he came back home he bought a boat and an outboard motor. His fishing skills were something to be envied. He declares: "I could go out on the water anytime I wanted to. I decided I would go ahead and sell some fish. I think I got 15 to 20 cents a pound for them and I probably sold 100 pounds a day. I did a lot of that kind of fishing for a while. Most people who know me down here know that I am the graduate on catching flounder. I'd have people call me from upstate New York and all around asking me how to catch flounder." Vernie learned his fishing skills from his father, also an avid fisherman. He misses the days when he first came here—the water was beautiful and clean, and you weren't restricted on how or where you fished. You could get oysters anytime you wanted and there were plenty of them.

One of the biggest changes to the area Vernie has seen is the golf courses that have been built everywhere. He understands the advantages of having the courses since they generate so much revenue from tourism, bringing in northerners and Canadians who think the climate is great year-round, especially for golf. However, he thinks the chemicals used to maintain the courses are polluting the water and ruining the fishing.

Vernie always remembers his childhood home fondly—where he fished and hunted, and how he helped out at his father's store. He says he has good memories of working with his father, "I can't remember any unpleasant part of my work at the store. We helped each other and we worked together."

Mason & Ginny Barber

Mason and Ginny Barber moved to Sunset Beach in 1986. They lived in Greensboro and were vacationing at Cherry Grove when they found Sunset Beach while exploring the area. They had friends who had come down and told them good things about Sunset Beach. They thought it had the reputation for being the best-regulated town on the North Carolina coast. They also liked the fact that Sunset Beach was not eroding as other beaches were.

Mason and Ginny were not strangers to moving. By the time they settled on the Waterway they had lived in twenty-four different houses. They both worked for Exxon Corporation and had traveled extensively over the southeast. When Exxon moved its headquarters to Houston, the Barbers didn't follow. They wanted to get away from big city living and try small town living. They built their first house on Canal Avenue as a vacation home in 1984 and lived primarily in their house in Greensboro. Mason retired in 1986 and thought it was crazy to keep two houses, so they moved to Sunset full-time.

He remembers that shortly after they bought the lot, someone in Greensboro told them that a new bridge was going to be built. They hadn't known, as the real estate people hadn't mentioned it. Mason went to Raleigh with a few friends and met with the highway department. He was assured that they would never build a bridge, but if they did, they would buy his house. Less than a year after their move to the beach they got a knock on the door. The State Department wanted to buy their property because they were going to put the bridge there. Apparently the bridge *was* going to happen. The Barbers began looking for another lot. The highway department gave them ample time to close the deal and to build a new house. They began building a new house in 1988 and moved the following year. After the purchase of the Barber's former home, the bridge planning hit a wall when an environmental impact study held up the processing and stopped the building for years to come. Since they liked their second house on the Waterway much better than the first, they really didn't mind having to move.

While building their new home, Mason became involved with the Taxpayers Association. At first, he was all for

keeping the old bridge. He later changed his mind when he saw how often it broke down. He ran for Mayor of Sunset Beach and won. He held the position from 1988 to 1995. Mason has a skewed vision of the politics that went into building this town—he made enemies, he made friends and most notably he made conflict. Mason describes the Taxpayers Association, which propelled him even more into the political scene at Sunset Beach: "When it first started, a lot of the residents joined, but when they found out that it was going to be a fight all the time they just dropped out. They didn't want anything to do with it."

As mayor, Mason spent most of his time sparring with Minnie Hunt and Ed Gore, but he also got a lot accomplished. When the median strip was overgrown with weeds, Mason tried to get the Taxpayers Association to clean it up. When that didn't work he went out and started pulling up weeds himself, toting buckets of water from his own house to water the grass. Another problem the county faced was garbage collection. The truck was old and kept breaking down, making the workers unable to collect garbage in the rain. Unaware of this problem, Mason received complaints about the garbage not being picked up one rainy afternoon. He went to the maintenance shed and found the men asleep. He went and bought rain gear and went back to the garage and said, "We *do* pick up garbage, now put this on!"

The rental tax he favored made it possible for the town to raise enough money to undertake a few projects. One was getting 9-1-1 service, and the other was arranging the deal for the parking area at the gazebo.

When the people of the town decided they needed a local grocery store, Food Lion agreed and wanted to be in the area where the Dollar General is now (specifically where the furniture store was). But the chain had serious concerns about being able to make it in a vacation area if they couldn't sell beer. So Mason said he'd fight for them to be able to sell alcohol if they'd get on board. Tom Smith was the C.E.O. of Food Lion at the time, and Mason and Ginny remember that he flew down for the grand opening and that people lined up just to shake his hand.

Ginny and Betty Waldmiller, started the Beautification Committee which began planting flowers and picking up litter around the area.

Mason helped to make Sunset Beach better in the only way he knew how, with old-fashioned hard work. Although he hasn't served as mayor in a long time, he still cares about this area. He has kept a close watch on the political "goings-on" in this town and has frequently made his environmental concerns for the area known, saying, "I am all for protecting the environment myself. I live here and have an investment here."

Dean Walters

While working in Myrtle Beach twenty-eight years ago, Dean Walters drove to the Sunset Beach area and, driving across the Ocean Isle Beach Bridge, was overwhelmed. He called his wife, Skipper, and told her that he had found a new place to live. This was in 1982. He bought a condo on the west end of Ocean Isle Beach and opened a small mortgage brokering office.

He says that at that time everyone met at the Island House, which was the center of activity, whether you were developers like Paul Dennis or Odell Williamson or a local plumber or contractor. Every morning you had breakfast at the Islander, and at night about 5:30, you went to the Island House—which was Victoria's and is now Bourbon Street—and had a drink. After a while, the regulars would invite you to their table. In those days, it took a while for outsiders to be accepted.

Dean Walters, whose claim to fame was going to school with Connie Chung and Goldie Hawn in Silver Spring, MD, says that nobody worked on Wednesdays back then. Everybody played golf at Ocean Isle Beach. In those days there were only about 100 people living at Ocean Isle. He adds that there was no one on the other side of Hwy.179.

Every Wednesday, a group would meet at Ocean Isle Beach and play golf. Paul Dennis was one of the leaders who always chose the teams. Paul noticed that Dean played a little better than the average player and, as Paul liked to win, he made sure that Dean was on his team as often as possible. That's when Paul pulled Dean aside and said, "You know, you seem to know a lot about golf courses." He found out that Dean, after graduating from Wake Forest, had been involved with building golf courses, remodeling them, and even running one in Charlotte. So he said, "You know, we finished Oyster Bay and it looks successful, and we're looking to do something else. Would you be interested in what we plan to do?"

Dean thought that was an interesting thing to think about. Dan Maples came and met with everyone, and

they all bought in because he had built Oyster Bay and was turning it into a huge success. The partners knew Dan because Oyster Bay was built on Sea Trail land and on some of Ed Gore's land. A relationship existed because Larry Young hadn't had enough money to build the whole course. Sea Trail agreed to take a second position so he could borrow enough to finish it. They built the lake that is to the right of hole #1 and a few other lakes on the backside of the course. Sea Trail fronted the money to develop those projects to help Larry make this thing go. All of a sudden it hit, and in 1983 Golf Digest proclaimed it The Resort Public Course of the Year. The guys Dean had been hanging out with were smart enough to see what was going on and say, "That's not so stupid after all; maybe that's a good idea."

Because the land had already been marked as home sites for stick-built cottages and mobile homes, same as Seaside Station and Shoreline Woods, this was a departure from the current development plan, so much discussion ensued before it was decided to build patio homes.

Dean can still envision Paul Dennis on a bulldozer at Seaside Station driving straight down the line, building streets just as straight as could be, and then returning to clear the land. You could come down on a Friday or a Saturday, choose a mobile home from the selection offered by Paul Dennis, John Williams, or Harris Thompson, pick out a lot, and come back the following weekend—that thing would be hooked up to sewer and water and you could walk right in and live in it. The next week, after putting 10% down and agreeing to pay the balance in 10 years at 10% interest, it would be "lights on." All that changed in 1986. The government decreed that the developers had to pay 30 to 40 percent taxes on the profits, so they couldn't take just 10% for the down payment anymore. So it was a good time for a departure from business as usual and a good time to sign up Dan Maples.

It was 1984 when they started and Dean told them if they liked what they saw, then pay him; if they didn't, then don't. There would be no hard feelings. He'd have fun with it. But he did insist on them buying him a

Top left is the first sign announcing Sea Trail's mobile home lots in Seaside Station. The price for a lot was about $3000 dollars and you could purchase one for $300 down and pay for the balance over 10 years with no credit check or closing fees. Note: the first Sea Trail logo which symbolized the old trail by the sea used by George Washington's coach.

At bottom left is the corner of Routes 179 and 904 at Seaside. Walgreens is now on the lower right corner and the CVS store is on the upper right corner. The lower left corner had wild grapes that the bears loved as evidenced by their tracks.

The photo above is typical of land now covered with golf courses.

4-wheel drive vehicle. During the next few years they bought several, most of which he wrecked.

Dean met Dan Maples and together they started laying out the course. Dean, who wasn't really looking for work, wasn't interested in the pay because he wasn't sure he wanted the job. He had other businesses and he was already doing what he wanted to do. He had retired at the age of thirty-six with the idea of accepting a "lesser life style." Maybe not playing as much golf as before, digging his own worms instead of buying them, and reducing his level of living to enjoy life more. But here he was agreeing to help build a golf course for these guys, as well as a clubhouse, and even hiring the staff.

Before they parted company that night Paul Dennis said he wanted to show Dean the spot he had selected for the clubhouse. He took Dean out in his "4-wheel drive" Lincoln Town Car and, after meandering around, pulled up and got out. He walked over, pointed, and said, "This is where I want to build the clubhouse." Dean remembers looking around and not being able to see a darned thing. It was so dark that the jackrabbits needed flashlights to find their holes. But Paul could see it all, saying, "This is the highest piece of land on this whole property and I am going to build the clubhouse here and you can build the golf course around it."

Over the next weeks and months they walked all over the land, excited to see it developing bit by bit. Dean says that things changed from the way Dan Maples originally planned #1, saying that he and his partners moved it down, and that #2 was actually up where the road is at Clubhouse Road. They moved it down to the water and dug out the extension of the Calabash Creek, adding that, "Of course, you could do that then; you sure can't do it now. I'll never forget, I had the Army Corps of Engineers there and Hugh Hines and I walked to where the wetlands were. It felt like twenty degrees below zero outside and nobody wanted to stay out too

The picture above shows one of the first buildings in the Seaside section of the Sea Trail commercial area under construction. The bottom picture shows its appearence today.

Golf courses abound in Sunset Beach

long. We went up around the grave yard and, where the #1 grave site was, there was a little road, an old logging road that went across right there and over to where Osprey Watch is—it went right across the creek. In the summer I could take my little car and drive right across it. In the winter, during the rainy season, there would be more water in it, of course. But I could actually drive right across to where the Osprey Townhouses currently are and make my way to the top of the hill there. The road kind of went right, then left, and if you went toward the right to about the middle of #15 fairway there was a huge sawdust pile. That was where Paul used to do some of his original sawmilling. We ended up using some of that for the greens on the Maples course. Sea Trail didn't own all the land across the way, on the other side, until it became available in 1986."

The Maples Golf Course was opened in 1985, after Dean hired the staff. The maintenance shed was where the old resort check-in was, just over a berm they had built. He remembers it being an exciting time as there was nothing this side of Hwy. 179 other than a little dirt road that was part of King's Trail, called King's Highway. It came down right about where the #10 cart path is on the Maples.

When 1,800 acres became available from International Paper, all of a sudden it was Sea Trail bidding against Odell Williamson for the rights to it. Paul and Dean went over to Odell's place and said, "Odell, this is stupid for us to keep bidding against each other." Odell said that he would love to develop the land with Sea Trail. There was some skepticism, but Sea Trail wanted the land so they said okay, they'd try it. And they agreed on a price—$3,000 an acre. When International Paper first bought the land from the Brooks, they paid 80 cents an acre. It was a huge difference from the first 11,000 acres that the Brooks sold them, and a hell of a lot of money back then. The only person who might have been able to compete with them was Sam B. Somersett. Luckily, he didn't even try.

There were maybe a hundred people living in Sunset Beach at the time and typically there wasn't a week when there wasn't a fish fry or cook out. Quite by accident, Paul Dennis and a couple of the developers started the Oyster Festival. They started cooking up some oysters at the airport at Ocean Isle Beach. Every week they were catching or making something and having a cookout. So, they were cooking oysters at the airport and pretty soon people started coming by. Then people started calling out, "Are you going to cook that again next year," wanting to know if they should make plans to come by again. In October, they set out barrels and tables

and it just developed. People came up and asked if they minded if they set out some crafts. Pretty soon it got so big it couldn't be held at the airport because of the parking. That was when Sea Trail volunteered their pavilion, which is now located to the right of the Conference Center. Next the festival was moved to the vacant lot where the old Food Lion would later be. It was there for a few years before moving to West Brunswick High School in Shallotte. It has since been moved back to Ocean Isle Beach, to the island side this time. What started out as a group of friends sitting around having a beer and eating oysters and spots turned into an annual fall festival that now draws over 30,000 visitors. Dean says it was a lot of fun.

Dean acknowledges that he's made some great mistakes in his life, and one of them was not writing down Paul's sayings. They had some interesting talks, especially when they were initially walking off the land. He says you can't imagine what it was like on the Maples #17 and #18. There were natural springs all through there, and they found what surely must have been the best stills in the county. Bottles, jugs, and beautiful jars were everywhere. They ended up burying them with dirt or destroying them by shooting them with a gun. According to the old timers, the main still was there, one of the centers where they made the home-brewed liquor that was carted down to the water's edge to be shipped out by skip or boat. They found several stills all along #18, nice sized ones—big ones. This was in 1984.

One day Paul and Dean were on #15 at Sugar Sands, named because it was pure and white and spun-fine like sugar, when Roy Gibson approached them about buying lots and building houses where the woods were. Dean thought the location along #16 was a great place for houses. The four principles—Ed Gore, Miller Pope, Harris Thompson, and Paul Dennis—had varying ideas. Ed Gore said there were other projects they could take on, ideas that would make Seaside Lakes, the name the course was originally incorporated under, more desirable. Harris Thompson didn't like the idea much because he was in the mobile home business. Ed and Miller were not. Miller didn't care, since developing property wasn't his field, but Ed Gore continued to harp on it. He finally got Paul and the others to listen to him. Eventually, Paul changed his mind, agreeing there was potential in Ed's plan, and the idea of building up those lakes like at Oyster Bay really appealed to him. He had an idea for one next to the #1 green. There was nothing more fun for Paul than building lakes and moving dirt. He would rather do that than anything. But the partners didn't want to build; they wanted other people to do that work. Finally,

it was decided to find a builder and let him do it. James Brown came from Albemarle where Paul was born and Paul was a partner with some of his family, so James Brown came and built "sugar shacks" in Sugar Sands. One of them eventually became Dean's home. With the golf course completed and opened for play in October of 1985, the development process continued. (As an aside, Larry Brown, James' brother, built Ed and Jody Hughes' house. Ed is the historian to whom this book is dedicated).

The partners decided they would buy the rest of the available land with Odell Williamson. After six months of bickering and accomplishing little, it was decided they needed to split up the property—it was just not going to work. Sea Trail was one of the few entities that could compete with Odell financially, but Odell wanted to drag his feet and, as long as he owned fifty percent, there was nothing anyone could do about it. So they agreed to meet in the office and divide the land. They would mark the lots and Odell would get first choice. Dean says, "Well you know that was a scary day," adding that, "Odell could have taken where the Jones course is and that would have been an interesting split. But I had a feeling from day one, and had even placed a dollar bet, that Odell would take 904 property, because he thought the value was in commercial property. Of course, he signed his name, and we split. The way everything went that day could have changed the entire course."

In order to split the number of acres, the land was cut off at Angels Trace. Part of Odell's settlement became Angels Trace Golf Course, which later became Mark Saunders' property, and is now Jaguar's Lair. Some of the Rice Mill section also went to Odell. There were fifty acres that are now part of the Byrd course, the 18th tee and the 8th green. There was a fifty-acre parcel that belonged to a black family and there was John Frink's property

which went all the way down to the Calabash Creek; but they were able to make a deal with all the people involved. The other part that was cut out, where Planter's Ridge is, was owned by Corbit Packing Company. They bought both pieces to put together the total package.

At this time Ed was building ten to twelve houses on the island with A.O. King, Al Morrison, and Don Safrit. The town members met in the Old Town Hall—including Francis Kanoy (the mayor at the time), Al Odom, Cathy and Joe Peed, and Carl and Mary Katherine Griffith. Dean says Sea Trail was treated as a stepchild, a truly different entity—as different as salt & pepper. There was no relationship at all. Of course, they weren't in the town at the time. So, they were entirely on their own, left to their own devises. The only one who could do anything for them was Ed.

The first thing that drew Sea Trail and the town closer together was legislation that allowed liquor to be bought by the drink at Sea Trail. Until then, if you dined out and wanted a drink with your dinner, you had to bring it with you. Butch Redwine introduced legislation that said any golf course in Brunswick County could serve liquor by the drink, whether they were in a municipality or not. At that point, Sea Trail didn't really care if they were in the town or not. At this time, nobody even lived in Sea Trail. The first owners didn't move in until 1987 or 1988. The first people were in Sugar Sands, known as "The Project" at that time. Then property was sold to get the Food Lion, and the expansion has continued ever since. The first parcel incorporated was a section of Sugar Sands and then the Maples Clubhouse.

Dean still owns a house in Sugar Sands; he rents it for six months at a time to homeowners who are building.

The reason he didn't stay? He says that people ran him away. They came to his door to ask questions, stopped him at street corners while driving, and generally made a nuisance of themselves. The defining incident came when he was in his yard raking leaves after church one Sunday. Three homeowners on bikes rode up and said, "Oh Dean, since you're here, let me talk to you about something . . ." He says he walked inside and told his wife Skipper, "We're out of here."

Dean remembers his partners fondly. He says the guys were all unique in their own way. He says Miller Pope is probably the greatest promotional person he's ever seen. "As a graphic artist this guy knows advertising, promotion, and how to write brochures. His brochure for The Winds brought more people than you can imagine. His verbiage and his ideas for promotions were truly professional. Miller was active on the Travel Counsel, with the North Carolina Tourist Association, and with Southeastern Tourist. He used to make trips as the Vice President. He would go to New Orleans every couple of months. He would bring people down from the North; he used to make everybody so mad (Paul and the other guys) because Miller would bring in all these people for free and then, of course, he would let Sea Trail pay for their dinner and golf. But these guys didn't understand what he was doing. He would turn around and get free ads in the papers, free articles in magazines, and all kinds of things like that. Miller is a wonderful promoter.

"John was the detail man. John Williams was a chemist by trade. He wanted to know everything. He would look at the financial statements. You got $70,000 in there for seed, $105,000 for chemicals, and $100,000 for fertilizer; and he wanted to know what this $57 bill is for the telephone. Let me tell you, that's what you need.

The board of a corporation that is small needs somebody like him.

"Paul Dennis was the leader and the visionary; he's not here anymore, he passed. He was married to Connie, Connie was a Frink. She's now on the board and she's kind of quiet. She's very committed to her church; it's her own church. She and Doris Redwine and some others run it. Paul was a smart man. He was a hard worker. But he was also good to the people who lived here. If you looked around, Paul was an example of a multi-millionaire who had friends. You don't always find that. Paul was the strong one and he made these guys money all the time.

"The other one, of course, is Ed Gore, Ed and Dinah. Ed has a lot of knowledge, he questions a lot of things. Ed fit in very well with the four-man board. In the last years he backed away as he had a lot to handle with Ocean Ridge. Ed was really in charge there, made all the decisions. Here he was 25% and he didn't really have the final say. In the last years, he had a lot on his mind with building his house.

"Harris Thompson had businesses, drugstores, convenience stores, stuff like that. His claim to fame was that he came down here and used money to buy land. Then he got into the mobile home business. He had the foresight to include Paul Dennis in some dealings. He actually set Paul up; he brought Paul into a lot of money.

"We were a two-class society in this area for a long time. You had the developers, who were Paul Dennis, Ed Gore, Odell Williamson, and Andy Anderson. Then you had everybody else. I am an oxymoron. I wasn't a developer but I made more money than a plumber. I was one of the few who were somewhere in the middle when I came here. It was truly a two-class society. Paul Dennis was one of the upper class who would rather associate with the other class than his own people, he was just that kind of person.

79

"Over the years that I have been here, it's been a good group, but Paul was definitely the final decision maker. They might argue in a meeting, they might disagree, but when the meeting adjourned we would all go to lunch and everybody would be happy—there wouldn't be anybody upset by this or that. Everybody would be fine."

Dean has great admiration for Linda Fluegel, Sunset Beach Town Administrator, saying that she is a true politician. "She was always able to have the council like her, one way or the other. She became stronger and more knowledgeable until she was really the only one who knew what was going on. Anyone new coming in had to rely on her for her knowledge of what was what, and of things that went on in the past. As you build a bigger organization, you look to someone who saves you work. Linda did that. Linda was the ultimate politician; she was always able to keep everyone satisfied."

Regarding Minnie Hunt, Clete Waldmiller, Jan Harris and others they associated with, he says they were always negative—all the time. The only positive things he remembers about Clete is that he and Mason Barber used to pick up trash. "There wasn't a day you wouldn't see Mason or Clete walking up and down the streets picking up trash. Minnie was just negative. Every time you were around her she was against you. She didn't like Sea Trail and she didn't like Ed Gore as he represented Sea Trail. And because of it, she didn't like me. She didn't like anything we were doing. She always wanted to be by herself, with her little group over there. They were always negative. They never said you've done a nice job over there at Sea Trail. The town was growing, and they never liked that at all."

Dean left Sea Trail in 2000, after eighteen years of developing it, some as President and CEO of the corporation. During his time at Sea Trail he was active in the community, serving as president of the Chamber of Commerce and Chairman of the Board of Brunswick Community College. During these past years, he has been involved in several developments in Brunswick County. Presently, Dean is completing his third, four-year

Top left: John Williams, Miller Pope, Ed Gore, and Paul Dennis (the Sea Trail Partners)

Top right: building the fairway on Jones/Byrd #10

Center right: clearing trees

Lower right: completing work on the Jones/Byrd Clubhouse and the Maples Clubhouse

Left: Dean Walters confering with Dan Maples and Ellis Maples

term as
Town Commissioner
at Ocean Isle Beach.

He dabbles in real estate and helps his son, Scott, with Coastal Pool/ PPM, Scott's successful pool service. He enjoys spending time with his ten grandchildren and two great grandchildren.

Reflecting on his experiences with the "Characters of Brunswick County" and with building what he believes to be one of the finest golf communities in the Southeastern United States with the finest homeowners, he says, "They will remain the highlight of my career."

The final purchase of land from International Paper led to Sea Trail Corporation hiring golf course architect Dan Maples of Pinehurst to build its first course (he also built Marsh Harbor and Oyster Bay). Renowned golf course architect Rees Jones (known for remodeling the U.S. Open Golf Courses) was hired to design the Rees Jones Course and, finally, Willard Byrd (who has designed a number of courses in the area), built the third and final course at Sea Trail. Several clubhouses followed, then the Carolina Conference Center, the commercial real estate center, and the medical facility. All leading to a well-planned, tight-knit community that Dean says is, "The finest bunch of homeowners on the East Coast!"

Left is the "Pink Palace." Shown above is a home in Seaside Station, the first development in Sunset Beach off the barrier island. Below is the Sea Trail('s) property owner's club house.

Hugh S. Munday

Hugh Munday moved to Sunset Beach in 1980. Sunset was starting to hit its developmental peak; new houses were sprouting up all over the place. There were about 700 houses already built on the island and another 500 or so that would be built over the next twenty years. Hugh was a builder from Lenoir, North Carolina. He came to Sunset Beach and began doing "spec" building. Everything he built was on the island or the Waterway. He avoided building on the mainland or in Sea Trail. He built the beach houses of several longtime residents, including Clete Waldmiller and Ray and Caramel Zetts. He initially lived in a house that belonged to Ed Gore. As he built houses, he moved into them, then sold them, and moved again. He now lives on 16th Street in a house that was moved from 13th Street—a house with some interesting history.

As an incentive for others to buy his lots and build houses on them, Mr. Gore gave a lot to a man who had done some work for him with the provision that he put a house on it. It was a marketing ploy that would pay off in the long run. At the time, Fort Bragg was demolishing old Army housing, including buildings that had been used as barracks. They were free to anyone who would move them. Hugh doesn't know how this particular building was taken apart or how it traveled over a hundred miles and was conveyed to the island, but there are clues all over the house that it was once split right down the middle. During recent renovations he found evidence of windows and doors that had been sealed off. The former enlisted men's quarters was deposited on the lot on 13th Street and became a beach house on what was then the east end of the island. That was before Mannon Gore finished dredging. The Fort Bragg house was eventually moved again, this time not quite so far—to the new end of the island, to 16th Street, where it is today.

Hugh built a few custom homes, but stuck to primarily building spec houses because custom homes didn't pay off. He quickly learned that building beach houses, living in them, and then turning them over was the ticket

to making it big in the area.

Regarding the permanent residents on the island, he says, "Let's say there are 1,200 houses here, at least 800 or more are under property management contract with one of the three firms on the island. There are only about 100 year-round residents on the island. So it all boils back down to the tourist and real estate business. Food Lion would dry up and blow away if it weren't for the tourists, although the population of the county is growing enough." He believes things are going to continue to grow in Brunswick County; the local Home Depot and other retail chain stores coming into the area are evidence of that.

While Hugh acknowledges that tourism is big business in this area, he thinks that the town and the property managers should be more involved with regulating the tourists. He describes a major problem faced by beach rental companies: "The issue was brought up by the health department. Ads used to say it sleeps ten or sleeps whatever, now they just tell you how many beds there are and that's it. As far as I know, nobody goes around and counts to see how many people are sleeping in those beds. Tourists have been squeezing as many people as they can into a rental for years now; and that many people can cause undue wear and tear on these rental properties."

Hugh is a little more laid back when it comes to tourists enjoying the beach itself. Many locals and beachgoers have complained in recent years about beach tents and cabanas being left overnight, to which Hugh replies, "What is the problem about walking around a tent? What if someone is lying there? You would walk around."

He is really proud that the bridge is being built because of the safety issues. He says he will miss the old bridge and that he never did mind waiting to cross it. He's very interested in the design of the new bridge and thinks that in the long run it's going to be good for the Waterway and marshes. He is pleased with the way the rainwater is going to be diverted, captured, and filtered so that the grease and oil from the cars does not contaminate the marshes as runoff. Hugh appreciates that the State is looking ahead and protecting the coast that he loves so much.

Ray & Carmel Zetts

Ray and Carmel Zetts left their home in Cleveland, Ohio to move to Sunset Beach in 1993. They had owned a condo and vacationed in Calabash since 1976, so when it came time to retire they thought of Sunset Beach. They bought the first house they saw and have been heavily involved in the community they've grown to love ever since.

After working long hours at Revco Drugs corporate office in Twinsburg, Ohio, Carmel thought she would go crazy with all the free time she now had on her hands. One of the things she did to occupy her time was attend a coffee every second Tuesday of the month on the island. At these coffees, where women of the island would gather and socialize, she met Minnie Hunt. Minnie was involved with a Sea Turtle Preservation group. Minnie took Carmel and another woman named Susan to the east end of the island to show them how they could help the sea turtles. Carmel was hooked.

Carmel, along with about fifty volunteers, scans the beach every morning from May through August for sea turtle nests. Between 5:30AM and 7:00AM she accompanies different groups as they survey the beach. She schedules people for different days and areas so that they won't get bored or burned out. They mark the nests with wooden stakes and tape them off to protect them from beachgoers. Sometimes they move a nest to a safer location, usually because the nest is below the high-water mark and is likely to get washed over.

Records for the Sea Turtle Watch program date back to 1989. It is completely funded by volunteer efforts through fundraising or contributions from the local business community. Carmel hosts training sessions for new volunteers and conducts seminars to inform people about the group and its efforts to protect the sea turtles in the area. Sunset Beach typically only attracts Loggerhead turtles and Leatherbacks, which can weigh up to 2000 lbs. She loves the work she does, but she could do without all the paper work. The program must keep records on the number of nests and the number of turtles, as well as G.P.S. locations and the species of the turtles. All of these documents go to the State Division of Wildlife. The group also deals with stranded turtles and turtles that wander onto land and become disoriented or hurt, in which case they transport the turtles to The Karen Beasley Sea Turtle Rescue and Rehabilitation Center at Topsail Beach.

Ray, a retired American Studies high school teacher, is not without his causes either. Years ago, when the island was overrun with cats and kittens, he took action by catching the cats and having them spayed and neutered with the help of veterinarian, Dr. Rabon. Ray negotiated a reduced fee for neutering and shots that the cats needed. Ray was part of a group that set up nine feed stations on the island. Volunteers donated about 120 pounds of food a week for the stations. The feed stations were so successful they branched out onto the mainland.

The Zetts truly enjoy their volunteer work, but they also enjoy their community. They both find time to fight for what's important, whether it's bridge conditions, terminal groins, or mandates for tourists who trash the beach. Carmel has no problem going to city hall and taking up her causes with the officials there. Ray sums up his experience at Sunset Beach by saying, "I think the relationship between the island and the people is a lot better compared to what it was when we first got here." He adds, "We just think it's a nice place to live. We enjoy living here. We enjoy the people."

Brian Dennis Griffin

Brian Dennis Griffin was not born in Brunswick County, nor did he grow up here. He moved here when he was fourteen to live with his grandparents, Paul and Connie Dennis. Paul Dennis, one of the four founders of Sea Trail Plantation, taught his grandson a few life lessons while showing him the ins and outs of the real estate business.

Brian, who started out working as a cart attendant at the Maples Golf Course, became familiar with the area fairly quickly. He learned that as a teenager there wasn't very much to do on a Friday night. "Our excitement was hanging out at the pier at Sunset Beach, just hanging out—that's it." He adds, "The biggest thing we used to do was go down to Myrtle Beach and cruise the boulevard. That's all we did, there was nothing to do around here."

He didn't get to enjoy those carefree teenage years for long before he got his start working his way around Sea Trail. While working as a cart attendant he went to the local community college and got his real estate license. Then he earned his PGA card and started working in the PGA program in the pro shop. From there he worked maintenance, mowed the greens and the common areas, worked the sand groves, and became the Personnel Director. After three years, his grandfather Paul came into his office on a Friday after the board meeting and said, "Monday you're going to start selling real estate."

Brian loves the real estate field. He says "I enjoy it, I think about my grandfather every day...I remember him being around here, just coming into my office or just sitting in the foyer. People would walk in and wonder who the old man was sitting there with the dress shoes and the shorts on with the Sea Trail shirt, his hair all messed up and dirty. They wanted to know who he was."

Brian became very close to his grandfather during the years he spent in Brunswick County. He can still rattle off sayings that Paul swore by. "He told me we were never too good to work with anybody," and "You always treat the help best." Paul served as a role model for Brian, who would later fill his shoes by stepping in to help run Sea Trail after his grandfather's passing. People loved Paul Dennis. They loved him because he was good to them. He made friends with everyone.

Paul Dennis was born and raised in Stanley County, in Albemarle, North Carolina. He was one of fifteen children in a self-proclaimed poor family. Brian recalls his grandfather describing his childhood: "He said he was so poor he couldn't even pay attention." They lived in a small two-room home where the kids slept six, seven, or even eight to a bed. Paul snuck into the Navy when he was seventeen and when he got out in his early twenties, he moved to Brunswick County. He lived in the Longwood area and began working in the timber business where he ran a sawmill. He eventually owned a mobile home business. In the 1970s, he and Harris Thompson set up an office in Shallotte. Before long, he and Connie, his wife who was a bank-teller, began buying up lots in the Seaside area. They'd save up and buy a piece of land, sell it, and then buy two pieces of land.

Paul teamed up with Miller Pope, Ed Gore, and John Williams to build their dream project—Sea Trail Plantation. "He really wanted to make Sea Trail work; he really wanted to make Sea Trail *the* place to live with the quality of life that everybody wanted," that's what he once told his grandson. The company was handed down to the children and grandchildren of the founders after Paul Dennis died and Miller Pope resigned. Brian explains the decision behind passing it off to the next generations. "We knew there were some talented individuals who would be able take it to the next level, nice people and young people. I really feel good about it. I just feel like we are still in the infant stage. We're going to see some commercial areas, some new buildings, and some new amenities that are really going to put us on the map."

Brian fondly remembers a story his grandfather told him a few years before he passed away. "He told me he loved to play in the dirt. I think that he told me he was in the 4th grade at the time and that he never did pay much attention in school. The teacher told him that if he didn't pay attention and get his education he was going to be digging ditches the rest of his life. 'My teacher told me that,' Paul said, 'but I have made a pretty good living digging ditches.'"

Larry & Cherry Cheek

Cherry Cheek and her family moved to Sunset Beach in October of 1986. They first came to Sunset Beach in 1975 for a vacation with friends who owned a house on 34th Street. They fell in love with the area and decided to build their own house on the bay side of the island in 1984. Cherry and her husband, Larry, had lived in Rockingham, North Carolina for several years. Larry had a successful dental practice, served on a bank board, and was president of the Cotillion. Cherry describes her life in Rockingham: "We were in all these social clubs and we were going to formals every other weekend. It was just overwhelming and both of us said we just don't want to do this anymore." They wanted to move right away so their boys wouldn't have to change schools and leave friends behind. With the idea of a slower paced life with their three children, the Cheeks set off for Sunset Beach.

Larry sold his practice in Rockingham and opened another in Calabash, with Dr. Deeb. Cherry kept the books for the dental practice, managed the office, and set up two houses—one on Sunset Beach and the other in Brick Landing. Her reason for having two houses in the area was that the boys were very young and she didn't want to be right on the water. Getting the boys to school from the island house also posed a problem when the bridge wasn't open. They stayed in Brick Landing until 1991 when they sold their house and purchased another on Shoreline Drive. They moved again in 1998 to a house they had built at Sea Trail. After a few years they sold it and bought another one in the Oyster Pointe section of Sea Trail. Cherry jokes, "When my corners get dirty I like to move." When Cherry and her family moved to the house on Shoreline Drive, she was approached by Mason Barber, who suggested she run for town council. Cherry, had become a bit of a "tabloid darling" in the area because of her work with the Chamber of Commerce and her community involvement, but had no experience in politics and no knowledge of what this would entail.

After some friendly coercion, Cherry ran for town council. She took office in 1992. In 1995, she ran for mayor and won. She ran again in 1997 unopposed. Cherry gained a new appreciation for the hard work and thought processes that go into politics. She adds, "There is a lot of thoughtfulness that has to go into every move you make in politics. You really have to look within yourself to decide if you're doing the right thing or not. I think that in those first few years, I realized that there were a lot of times people wanted to influence you to do things that may not be exactly what you wanted to do, and I tried to make it a practice to do what I felt was right." One of the precedents she set, for herself and for subsequent mayors, was an open door policy. She opened up Town Hall for people to come in to talk face-to-face.

While Cherry was making waves as mayor, Larry was working hard at making his dental practice a success. He found himself left out of decisions concerning the practice after Dr. Deeb brought on another dentist, Dr. Fanning. Losing ground on decision-making in his own practice became difficult for Larry, and after fourteen years of never taking a day off and never taking a vacation, he decided to retire.

As mayor, Cherry faced some criticism and she has certainly been subject to the rumor mill, but she has always made her priorities clear. Her family always came first. She describes the problems she faced trying to manage her job and her time with her family, "Because of the amount of time that we spend with our children and the time that I had to spend working and going to meetings, it really cut into a lot of my personal time with my husband and our friends. So, what we basically had to do was drop out of doing so much socializing and spend more time with each other and with our children. We will get back around to the socialization sometime later on in life." The Cheeks' boys are now grown and making their own waves in the world, and Cherry and Larry finally have time to slow down and enjoy the beach they moved to be near. Cherry has high hopes for Sunset Beach and its future development, "Ideally, I would love to see sidewalks, bicycle paths, and places where people could walk and visit without having to get in the car and drive. I would love for it to become a town that looks like something from the 50s, a place that is friendly and open, where people can walk in the evenings, find a place to sit, and have lemonade while visiting with neighbors. That kind of thing, I think, it would be great."

Marcel & Jan Lawson Wright

Jan and her first husband, Marcel Lawson, used to live in Charlotte where Marcel worked at Jimmy Sanderford's dealership repairing cars. He taught mechanics at Robertson Tech in Lumberton prior to that, and Jan worked for the trucking division of Western Auto in Gastonia, maintaining the fleet of trucks, ordering parts, and familiarizing herself with the lingo. So they both knew trucks, and they both knew cars, and they both knew a lot about the repair business.

They began coming to Sunset Beach for vacations and each time, they found it harder and harder to make the drive back. On one such drive, Marcel said, "You know, there's no place there to have a car fixed. We should open a repair shop." Jan didn't think anything of it because she didn't think he was serious at the time. But he soon proved that he was. They moved down to the beach in 1988 and opened Seaside Auto Service in 1989—the year of Hugo and the year of the infamous Christmas snowstorm on the coast.

Marcel was the mechanic and Jan was the bookkeeper, maid, and head "go-fer"—running head gaskets to Laurinburg, picking up parts in Wilmington, and dropping people off at the beaches while their cars were being worked on. The shop was located in the strip mall across from The Village at Sunset. They started the business without knowing whether it would be successful or not. Jan placed ads in *The Beacon* and did some radio ads, but she thinks the only thing that really helped was word-of-mouth.

Soon Marcel had earned a reputation as an outstanding mechanic, who was more than fair with his prices, and things took off. The first year they lived in North Myrtle Beach, but soon they discovered that the traffic they encountered going back and forth during the summer months was not at all convenient and they bought a mobile home at Seaside Station.

Jan remembers that they were at Topsail Beach visiting her sister on Christmas Eve when the snow began. As odd a sight as it was, they quickly realized it was not stopping anytime soon, so they left for home. They drove all the way through Wilmington with only one lane open and felt that they were very fortunate to have made it back. The snow kept coming and coming and soon everything was buried waist-high. It was ten days before people could get out. Many complained that the streets weren't cleaned (mostly people from the North, she adds), but how could they be—there were no snowplows!

Things were going really well for Marcel and Jan and their repair shop until a fateful night, November 16, 1995, when fire consumed and destroyed the shopping center. She remembers that William "Bookie" Taylor, who owned the complex (he also developed Hidden Valley and the area behind the post office), came and pounded on their door at 2:30 in the morning, yelling for Marcel to get up and get the cars out of the fenced-in area behind the shop. The big concern was the commercial trucks with full fuel tanks parked close to the buildings. But Marcel was not able to get into the office to get the keys as it was already consumed by fire when they arrived.

Jan says there were fire trucks everywhere. Every company within twenty miles responded—Sunset Beach, Calabash, Shallotte, Ocean Isle, North Myrtle Beach, Little River—but the fire had already spread across the roof and was fully involved when most of them got there. "At least no one was hurt," Jan says.

Stuart Cooke's personal truck burned completely and Jan remembers that he was so nice about it. And Jack Cain's vintage Corvette was there being repaired too. He was in Raleigh at the time and everyone was afraid

to tell him. But when they did and he came to see the damage, she said he was so good about it saying, "It needed a new paint job anyway." Jan and Marcel had a classic Chrysler from the 40s that Marcel was always toying with that could not be salvaged.

There were thirteen businesses in the strip mall including Nations Bank, Jack's Lock Shop, Tompkins Surveying, an embroidery shop, Ken Bridges office (a local attorney), and Turnage Heating and Air Conditioning. The High Tide Bar and Grill was at the end, where it's believed the fire started. Only two or three businesses had insurance and the auto repair shop was one of them.

Nations Bank had a firewall so it suffered minimal damage and was reopened "in no time," the others weren't so lucky: Jack of Jack's Lock Shop managed to get all his stuff out before the fire got to his store; the owners of the High Tide Bar and Grill lost everything as did most of the others; the woman who owned the embroidery shop was out of town at the time and didn't even know about the fire for a week; Bookie Taylor had no insurance but vowed to rebuild, promising a January time frame, but things were held up for almost a year by other people's insurance companies. The renters who had insurance were told they had to produce records and inventories and, of course, all that had burned in the fire. Marcel and Jan were insured, but had none of the required paperwork. So they did not see any money for over a year and the amount they received was quite a bit lower than they'd expected. Their service shop was not totally destroyed; they had some inventory consisting of tires, Freon, oxygen, chemicals, and an assortment of parts such as starters, fuel pumps, belts, batteries, and brake and starting fluids. But there were no tools and there was no place to work, so they were not able to reopen for a very long time.

Fletcher, from Calabash NAPA came to help haul off some of the burned out vehicles and heard a cat meowing. "Girl," the stray cat Jan and Marcel had adopted, had been missing since the fire and it was assumed she had run away. But they found her under some bushes toward the back of the lot. "She had probably been unconscious for days," Jan says. She wrapped her in a blanket and took off to Dr. Ward's veterinary office in Calabash. All four paws were burned, as well as her whiskers and patches of hair. She was dehydrated and in shock. Dr. Ward said she was one tough "Girl" and kept her for a few weeks to make sure she was going to be all right.

While Marcel and Jan waited for the insurance money, several of their suppliers were gracious enough to buy back the products they had previously sold them. Among them were Ocean City Chevrolet, Jones Ford, Advance Auto, and NAPA. Fletcher, from NAPA, even took the time to come and pick up his products, leaving them a hefty check. The Sea Trail and Shoreline Property Owners Association took up a collection. With careful budgeting and help from friends, they were able to start putting their life back together.

Then one day, Tom Pope's father-in-law, Les Brady, took them to see a property on Route 179. By a bizarre coincidence, it was owned by Jimmy Sanderford, the owner of the dealership Marcel had worked for in Charlotte. They were able to make a deal and Jimmy even agreed to let them make payments to him. So . . . they were back in business. All their friends came and helped clear the land and do some remodeling on the building. Volunteers even did some electrical work to get them up and running. They found a way to get Marcel the new tools he needed, and placed a few ads in *The Beacon* to let folks know that they were up and running again. But, again, word-of-mouth is what brought the customers in. The hardest thing, Jan recalls, was getting insurance again and the insurance company even wanted them to buy flood insurance this time. The fact that she got scared every single time she heard a siren was a bit hard to deal with though.

Jan chuckles as she remembers the checkbook they found among the debris. The bank said that as long as all the numbers were there they could use them, so with charred edges, Jan began paying the bills with them. Kelly, at NAPA, used to joke when they brought in a check, "Got another one of those hot checks, huh?"

In 2000 Marcel started getting sick and ended up at Duke Medical Center where they were told he wasn't going to make it. Jan remembers how surprised she was when so many of his customers made the long trip to visit him. He died a week later under the care of hospice.

Jan followed Marcel's plan, sticking to everything they had discussed before he'd passed. He had insisted she sell the business and get away from all the work and worry. Jan says they were fortunate to have so many wonderful friends, almost all generated from their customer base. Marcel's mother, who is now 95, says that, "The best thing he (Marcel) ever did, was move to the beach."

Julia Thomas

Julia Thomas moved to Sunset Beach in 1980 after buying property in 1978. Julia and her husband, Lonnie, were living in Garden City just south of Myrtle Beach. Julia spent her time teaching gymnastics and judging competitions. Her husband was in the textile industry, and before they moved to Sunset Beach he suffered a heart attack and underwent major surgery. Lonnie never fully recovered from the heart attack and was unable to go back to work. His retirement was the final push that got them to move full-time to Sunset Beach.

Julia and Lonnie moved into Sea Trails on Indigo Circle (Shoreline Woods area off of Shoreline Drive), and soon after Julia became heavily involved in the community. She, along with other locals, formed a community organization that served the residents of Sea Trails (Seaside Station area is still referred to as Sea Trails by some) and the nearby area. Members would keep a lookout for each other's property when they were out of town and pick up trash scattered about the area. Julia was elected the first president of the group.

She says of the club's early days, "The first meeting was held at my house, then afterwards we met every month at the fire department and paid them so much each time we used it." The members had the organization incorporated and later adopted the title of Sea Trails Property Owners Association. Sea Trail Plantation donated the land and $5,000 toward materials for their homeowner's clubhouse on Station Trail. They had potluck dinners at least once a month, cookouts throughout the year, and arranged trips to places such as Brookgreen Gardens. In the early 90s when a Brunswick County baby, Jessica Clemens, was born without eyes they answered a need and raised over a thousand dollars for her care. The organization is now responsible for keeping up with the communal area known as Sea Trails. They had their 20th anniversary on September 28, 2002. Of the original twenty-six members, fifteen were still there.

Julia maintained a scrapbook of pictures of the members socializing and of the clubhouse being built, from groundbreaking to the finishing touch—a community painting party. In it is a letter from Property Owners Association President Zane Winters thanking Mr. Ed Gore and Mr. Paul Dennis for using their heavy equipment to clear the local roads during our "Once in a 100-year snow fall" in 1989, at Christmastime. Several residents had needed special attention or had to take trips for dialysis at Myrtle Beach, and while they had drivers, they needed tracks in the snow to get started.

Julia's community involvement didn't stop there. She was one of the founding members of the Sea Trail(s) Garden Club—a beautification program that planted flowers at the entrances of Sea Trail(s). Julia also went back to work part-time at a gift shop on the island, screen-printing t-shirts. In 1982, her husband Lonnie passed away. A few years later she met and married Jack. She and Jack became involved with the local fire department. At first, Julia started by writing the annual letter to the town but soon after, she and Jack learned to dispatch. She says of her volunteer work, "It got left on us. That's before 911 was here you see. So anytime day or night that a call came in, we had to be ready. There was one other man who had been in the service and knew the codes. I had to learn them, all the dispatching codes. That's how we got so interested in the fire department." They continued working with the fire department and were dispatchers for five years.

Julia became even more involved in the community in 1988 when she ran for town council. She was in office for eight years. She ran for office because she felt so passionate about the Food Lion situation the town was facing. She gives her reasons for wanting the Food Lion in Sunset Beach, "Many of the retirees didn't like having to drive all the way to Shallotte at that time or to Little River. And why should we give our tax money to Little River on our groceries when we could give it to our own state? I felt it would be a good thing for the community."

Julia was also elected the chairman of the Christian Education Committee for her church. She certainly gave a lot of herself to a town she came to love. She recalls, "I never worked so hard in my life as I had when I came here."

Joe & Carol Santavicca

Carol and Joe's migration south is typical of the way retirees find their way to Sunset Beach. They came for a long weekend with friends in the fall of 1993. Back in Burke, VA, they all carpooled, so they called their weekend an off-site meeting. The guys played golf and the girls shopped in Myrtle Beach. Carol decided that day that they were going to buy here. It was paradise; there was plenty of golf for him, and for her, there was the beach and all of the quaint little shops.

They contracted for a Club Villa in Sea Trail in January and by February they'd signed up their first renters. She remembers that their daughter, who had just graduated from college with an interior design degree, earned her first commission decorating their condo.

They moved to Sunset Beach in the spring of 1999 and started looking for a house, deciding to keep the villa for rental income and as a place for their family when they visited. On April 1, 2000 they moved into their lovely Thomas Kinkade-style cottage in the woods at Bonaparte's Retreat II.

In 2005, at the height of the real estate boom, they sold the condo. Carol served nine years for the POA and six years for the Town of Sunset Beach Planning Board and is now on the Sunset at Sunset Committee. She is devoted to the Sunset Beach Community and always eager to help out the local charities—once even volunteering herself and Joe as traveling chefs for gourmet dinners.

Carol says they love the area and the people. It's a comfortable area to move into as most of the people moving here are looking for a change of lifestyle, not looking to bring their lifestyle with them. "Except for those few, who make it harder on themselves to fit in," she adds with a knowing look.

Joe likes that there's parking everywhere—and no traffic. Adding that it's a comfortable living; there's not a lot of tension conducting your day-to-day business here.

Seventeen years after their first "off-site business meeting," they are still one of the happiest couples I know, living each day to the fullest and being the best ambassadors for our growing community.

Ken Buckner

Born in Ohio and raised in Michigan, Ken was educated at the University of Michigan and then went on to graduate with honors from the prestigious Art Center College of Design in California. He traveled to London for a year of fine art studies in the student room of the British Museum. Before moving to the N.C. coast in 1976, he worked for several large advertising agencies in New York and Los Angeles, owned an advertising art business, and created logos and ads for Bill Blass, Cole of California, and Pendleton. In Connecticut, he did photography for SAAB of Sweden, painted large oils for a multi-national corporation and portraits which included the grandson of Alfred Bloomingdale. Ken met Miller Pope when he was an illustrator in Westport.

Moving to the Carolina coast in 1976, he built a studio/home near the sea and painted, photographed, and experienced the beauty of his newly found paradise. He created large low-relief wood sculptures for the clubhouse atriums of Sea Trail and Ocean Ridge, and over 100 more for private beach homes. Today, he is known for his beach photos of timeless beauty.

He began teaching watercolor painting at Brunswick Community College where he met and later married UNCW graduate, artist Terry Sellers. Ken says, "She is intelligent, beautiful and unbelievably talented." They designed and built Doe Creek Gallery, located on thirty secluded acres of Sellers family land off Highway 17 in Supply. After twenty-five years together, they have had a "friendly parting of the ways" and the gallery, which offered their creations, is no longer open to the public. It is now used as a working studio that you can visit online at www.doecreekgallery. com. Terry is, "One of the most successful portraitists in the country." (American Artist Watercolor Magazine, 2007)

Ken first visited this area in 1974, at the urging of Miller Pope when they were working together in Westport. He thought it so beautiful that he bought six acres of land on Old Shallotte Road.

He could not believe that there was an undeveloped barrier island within a bike ride of his property. Miller told him about Bird Island while they were in Westport, but he hadn't believed him. Seeing Bird Island and Brookgreen Gardens confirmed his decision to move here. He notes that Brookgreen Gardens, established in 1931, is the largest American sculpture garden.

On July 4, 1976 Ken declared his creative independence by skinny-dipping on Bird Island. He assures me that absolutely no one was around. He destroyed his American Express Card and, in honor of his hero, Thoreau, lived without electricity for two years, two months and two days. "All I needed was a hand pump, propane stove and hand tools for building a small studio/home." The man who once had a thriving advertising art business in Beverly Hills and lived on the Southern California oceanfront now embraced simplicity. "My air conditioner was the ocean breeze under a shady pier and my Jacuzzi was the warm water rushing in and out of the island inlets. The sun and moon lit my beautiful new outdoor studio and the birds and wind through the pines provided the music. I felt that a great wealth had been bestowed upon me in the form of time and creative freedom—and it was tax free!"

Ken says you could see the Milky Way clearly at night back then. He used to sit on the beach over a campfire with old fishermen in the middle of the night, listening to their stories and waiting for the tide so they could bring in the nets. "There were a trillion stars in the sky," he exclaims. Then he chuckles, "I got paid in fish to help." He adds that, "they were very particular about the fish they kept, but the throwaways were damned good!"

He discovered that the most beautiful light occurred at sunrise and sunset and that it was impossible to paint it from life. Photographs, composed like paintings, became his main medium for creating images of beauty. He also enjoyed being out in nature much more than painting in his studio. Before discovering Sunset Beach, he thought

Carmel was the ideal—the perfect place to photograph sunsets over the ocean—and he often captured the foam dancing in the setting sunlight. But Sunset Beach knocked that out of the box as far as he's concerned. Of Sunset Beach, he states: "This place is unique. It is better than Carmel because it has the best variety of sunsets due to its geographic situation. Carmel has surf. Sunset has surf, sunset, and clouds . . . the clouds are very important here. The sand being flat is a huge bonus; I've never seen any place like it. At low tide it faces west and acts as a mirror, so that whatever is going on up above is duplicated down below, reflecting the amazing light and cloud formations." He adds that, "It really makes spectacular pictures." His photo on the cover of this book illustrates that exactly.

Ken says Bird Island provides the perfect background because no man-made structures intrude on the timeless quality he's after in his nature photography. He says he has never seen light as it is here, low and golden because of the influence of the ocean. And the Carolina blue skies in the winter beautify all the colors under them. It's when no one is around; no one is here to see these things in the winter.

He makes it his mission to bring us nature's beautiful palette against one of nature's most magnificent backdrops. Ken enjoys being out with the light in the early morning or late afternoon. He says half an hour before and half an hour after sunset or sunrise is the perfect time. There's no way you can paint it; it can only be photographed, which is why he switched to photography. You can see him off-season, from October to March or into early April, taking advantage of the high-flying clouds. He tries to go often as he says the more he goes, the better chance he has to get something rare.

Brookgreen Gardens is another oasis of beauty for him and his photos of the gardens and sculptures have a place of honor in their gift shop. Although he loves tobacco barns and all things rustic, "People come for the beach and want photos that remind them of the beauty and wonderful time they have here." Odell Williamson once told him, pointing at the ocean, "Son, that's the golden goose out there."

Ken loves the serenity he's found here. He has a new home erected on the same spot that the original studio occupied. He spends his time creating photos and living the simple life. He likes living in nature, apart from the rest of the world. He uses, "A little electricity but no credit cards or cell phones. I'm not a hermit but I do protect my creative time. Think Thoreau with a computer and digital camera." He says, "Today, technology is available that allows creative freedom and quality reproduction that was impossible a few years ago."

He says that at one time he lived on the ocean in Marina Del Rey and was making so much money he didn't have time to do more than throw checks into a drawer. But it soon became apparent that the quality of his life was diminishing. Because he's such a perfectionist, he wasn't enjoying his art as much as he wanted to. He wanted to create more meaningful art.

So he moved to the coast and built his home taking advantage of materials he found there. He collected decking that washed up after storms and used it to build his own deck. The one-time well-heeled man-of-the-hour is very happy living as a reclusive pauper, as long as he has his beach.

When he first came here he did limited edition, signed and numbered watercolors, but admits that painting got killed by photography, and digital photography is burying it even faster. Ken is a world-renowned photographer, but few people know what an exceptional painter he is. If you have an original painting by either Terry or Ken, it would behoove you to hold onto it.

As Ken wanders his thirteen acres of nature trails that meander through 100-year old pines and sits by his large water lily pond (named Walden Two) he muses, "Happiness is the most important bottom line."

His first book, "Favorite Beach Photos," will be available in 2010. Primarily photos of the South Brunswick Islands and, in particular, Sunset Beach, the book includes some stories behind the pictures.

For more information see his website: www.doecreekgallery.com

Nivan & Frances Milligan

Nivan Milligan was born in 1925 at Shallotte Point. He has lived in Brunswick County his whole life; he moved from Shallotte Point to Sunset Beach in 1958. Nivan worked as a painter and went to Ash, ten miles away from Route 130, to get a job. But it turned out to be too long of a trip with no car; it took most of the day just getting there and back. He met Frances while on a painting job and, after marrying, they decided to do something else. When Nivan and Frances moved to Sunset Beach, they bought a lot on the corner right before the bridge and began building their home and their store. He bartered with Mannon Gore for two pieces of land next to the old Sharks store. In exchange, he would build a motel for Mannon. Besides the Gores, the Milligans were the first people to live at Sunset Beach. At that time, there was no bridge, not even a ferry to shuttle people to the island. According to Nivan, there were no houses on the beach so there was no need for a bridge. However, the bridge opened later that year and, because of it, building started over on the island.

Nivan and Frances opened their store, Twin Lakes Grocery, in March of 1958. Most of the customers were people working and clearing land in the area. There were only a few families so the store catered mostly to the workers and the occasional fisherman. Nivan began doing contracting work in the area, while Frances managed the day-to-day operations of the store. When the town had grown to roughly thirty families, Nivan was elected town clerk. The town became incorporated in 1963 and, of the thirty people in town who could vote, six were elected to office. The first

election counted 29 votes. Those votes weren't necessarily from people who lived in the town either. In order to vote you only had to own a lot, and there were a few people from Wilmington who owned lots.

Nivan remembers his early days as town clerk citing, "We didn't have anything to do! I don't think we even had a tax at that time." His salary for holding the office was a whopping $50 a year. But he says people in town at that time didn't need money. "We didn't need it, we ate fish—we didn't have to have money 'til the Yankees came down here." In fact, while building up property on the island, Nivan said they built the houses and the hotel by swapping out the labor for lots up near his store.

The Milligans owned Twin Lakes Grocery for twenty-three years, often shuffling into side businesses such as running the 77 Sunset Strip Motel on the island and building pier houses. Nivan became a builder and a contractor for Sunset Builders, where he worked for several more years.

Nivan reminisces about the days when Sea Trail was a good hunting ground for squirrels. He says there used to be all kinds of wildlife in that area: turkeys, foxes, even deer. He remembers an incident when a deer came running across from the Waterway and saw its reflection in the sliding glass door. The buck ran right into it and knocked himself out. He reflects on his time in Sunset Beach, "We've seen this whole thing, the beach, and all this . . . Sea Trail—everything's been built up since we've been here."

The Kindred Spirit Mailbox

The weathered "post office" by the sea has been operating for almost thirty years now. What started as a tribute to the beauty and solitude of Bird Island is now an established landmark that thousands of nature lovers visit annually. Hundreds of photographers and artists have trudged to the west end of the island to capture the essence of the mysterious mailbox tucked high in a sand dune, and many a beach walker has rested on the roughhewn driftwood bench. Yours truly has even penned a romantic murder mystery centered around the Kindred Spirit Mailbox.

Before a sand-shifting storm in late 1997 filled in Mad Inlet, you had to use caution when venturing to the spit of land known as Bird Island. Beachcombers have been stranded by the tide because they were drawn to the mailbox and the wonderful letters left inside, begging to be read.

Notebooks, pens and pencils are kept in the mailbox, replenished by a team of secret volunteers, so that visitors can leave messages while they sit and enjoy the sights and sounds of the waves crashing on the shore. It is an unlikely post box, but over the years the exchange of thoughts and ideas has filled hundreds of notebooks.

The messages often express the writer's utter contentment with the paradise found here, with the serene beauty of the place, and with the unspoiled wilderness they can count on finding, year after year. Others delve deep into feelings, sharing emotions that run from overwhelming grief to young, exuberant love. It is a favorite place for men to kneel to present their sweethearts with rings. It is a cathartic place to search your soul and purge your thoughts.

Folklore has it that a woman from western North Carolina came up with the idea of the mailbox. Others argue it was someone from New Hope, or possibly a lady from the Sandhills or Lake Waccamaw region. Over the years, the mailbox and its upkeep have been credited to many people; Frank Nesmith being the one most locals favor as he helped plant the first Kindred Spirit Mailbox (it's had to be replaced a few times) in 1981. But it's fitting that the "Kindred Spirit" be a mysterious someone who diligently collects the books, then lovingly pores over each one before saving it as a valued treasure from the sea. The anonymity going both ways makes it particularly nice and lends to the mystique.

People have asked what has become of the notebooks that have been collected throughout the years. Several have expressed the desire to own a collection of the poignant notes and ramblings. I can tell you that, having read through many of the notebooks over the years, it would be an awesome task to catalogue even a small percentage of the messages. They are written by different hands, some barely legible due to handwriting and humidity, and they are written in a vast array of languages. And of course, there is no continuity as each missive is either a letter of gratitude, a plea of surrender, a heartfelt prayer, a poem of love, thoughts of desolation, a tribute to a loved one, plaguing inner thoughts, or full blown stories that span page after page after page . . .

How do you get to the Kindred Spirit Mailbox? Due to the acceding nature of the beach and some recent storms, the mailbox is now located in the dunes about a mile and a quarter past the last public beach access at 40th Street. It is close to a pole, but not the tall flagpole you'll come to first (remember, things are constantly changing at the beach, and the pole as well as the mailbox could be a victim of the next hurricane). It is about an hour walk. So put on your Nikes and *Just do it!*

The Ingram Planetarium

"Why is there a planetarium at Sunset Beach?" Many ask Scott Kucera this question as he hands them a ticket to the digital Sky Theater.

Ingram Planetarium is one of twelve planetariums in North Carolina. This is not a major metropolitan area, there is no university acting as a parent organization, and until recently the building stood alone, in the middle of a field surrounded by longleaf pines, turkey oaks and nesting osprey. Scott's initial response is, "Why not?"

He launches into his five-minute "elevator speech" and answers visitors before they slip into the dimly lit, 85-seat theater to watch amazing, high-definition digital programs about space.

As with most non-profit organizations, the Planetarium in Sunset Beach is the result of one individual's

Stuart & Louise Ingram

passion to serve the community in a way that's never been done before. Stuart Ingram had already succeeded in establishing the Museum of Coastal Carolina on Ocean Isle Beach that inspires people to learn more about the unique natural history, culture and environment of the coastal Carolinas. Ten years later, he decided to apply his experience as a World War II navigator and bring the wonders of the stars to Brunswick County residents and visitors.

Stuart passed away just as his dream was ready to take flight. He was able to see the Spitz 1024 Star Ball project on the 40-foot dome although the seats were not yet installed. It must have reminded him of sitting peacefully in the sand, on a south-facing beach in Brunswick County, gazing at the bejeweled night sky overhead.

Since 2002, the Ingram Planetarium has been serving students, families, and senior citizens at the rate of 15,000 visits per year. After installing the world's third SciDome HD digital projector (as pictured below) in 2009, there have been record crowds enjoying planet fly-bys, cosmic visualizations, and a spectacular perspective of our Milky Way Galaxy from more than 200-million light years away.

Coming out of the dome after a show, the Sky Theater-goers are smiling, some are asking questions, and some are shaking their heads in amazement at what they've just discovered about the universe we live in.

If you have ever gazed up at a magnificent starry night over the coastal Carolinas, then you know why Stuart wanted everyone to have a better understanding of astronomy. And if you haven't, then plan a trip inside the Sky Theater at Ingram Planetarium so you can better understand *your* place in the universe.

Scott Kucera is Executive Director of the Ocean Isle Museum Foundation, Inc., a non-profit organization that operates the Museum of Coastal Carolina and the Ingram Planetarium.

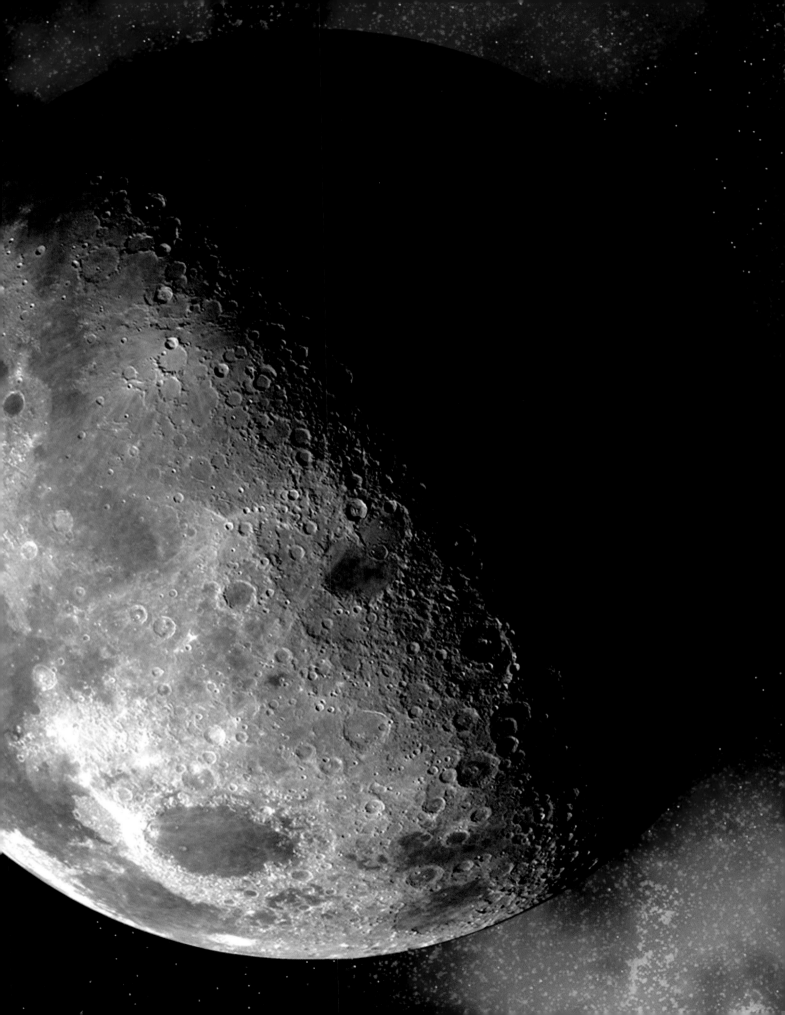

Sam B. & Marie Somersett

Sam B. (Bunn) Somersett remembers this place when it was nothing but dirt. He says of the area where he grew up, "It was dirt, all of it was dirt, there was no road then—there was no road to the landing (Somersett Landing), nothing but old dirt paths." Sam is one of the few who can remember a time before Ed Gore came and started scooping up land and developing property left and right. Sam's family has been in Brunswick County for longer than anyone can remember. His father's family—the Somersett side—used to own a farm where Ocean Ridge is now located. Sam was born there and he once owned all the land that is now Ocean Ridge Plantation. He says it changed hands several times before Ed Gore purchased it in the mid-80s.

Sam built his first house at Somersett Landing and in the late 50s or early 60s he built another house behind Bill's Seafood (which he owned for a time). Sam wore a number of hats, including construction worker. He was an ace at clearing lots. He also worked with Mannon and Ed when they were developing the island. He says: "That bridge cost me two lives (the equivalent of) waiting to get across it." He owned 17 trucks for hauling dirt and they were always waiting to get across the bridge. He also owned Coastal Hardware on Highway 904, ran a fish business, and he did construction on the roads for the county. *When did he find time to sleep?* Although he was primarily a builder, Sam is probably better known for his fishing. He says, "Cash wasn't a big deal then. I was in the dirt business and I was just down there running the seafood." They had what he called "surf" sand. They caught fish on the backside of the beach, "Then pulled them out and loaded them up."

Sam has pictures of himself standing in front of a big pickup truck full of mullet. He was a man who knew how to fish. He also had an oyster shucking plant next to Bill's Seafood. They shipped bushels of oysters to Baltimore, Farmburg, Florida and all over Maryland. His operation consisted of himself and a few guys who would help him drive to deliver his catch. They would also travel along the coast to fish, going to places like Morehead City and Virginia Beach. He laughs when he thinks about his business plan, "We caught the fish and turned around and sold it right back to the same places we caught it from."

One of Sam's more poignant memories about living in Brunswick County was the night Hurricane Hazel swept up the coast and caused major chaos in the area. He describes the night Hazel wreaked havoc on his family's store, "I had been fishing all night that night when Hurricane Hazel came by and I come in and went to bed about four o'clock. My momma called me up about nine o'clock and said. 'You'd better get down to your daddy's.' He had a grocery store down on the landing at what's now Pelican Point. She said the water was four-

feet deep inside the building. So I got up and went down there where he was and I told Pop, 'You better get out of here,' he said, 'No, it's just a northeaster.' I ain't never seen water this high. It kept right on coming so we left and come out here to Old Shallotte Road to the old school house. When they got back to the store they saw that the water had destroyed everything, they lost everything they had."

Another memory that stands out was the time alcohol came to Sunset Beach. This was a milestone for a small town in a once-dry county. Sam voted for the ABC store to come to Sunset Beach. He owned a small store at Sunset that was run by a friend named Rufus, and Sam had to sign papers so that they could sell beer in the store. The battle of the ABC store coming to Sunset was a hot issue that had everyone picking sides.

Sam was aware of the problems and situations that Ed Gore and Odell Williamson were caught up in, but he tried to stay clear of all of it. He says about the night Frank Nesmith cut Ed's tires, "I had left or just left (to move back to Grissettown) but I heard about it, everybody heard about it. Ed went looking for Frank when he found out who did it (took down his fence), and they both got bloodied up quite a bit. He (Ed) went to jail." Although Sam and Ed grew up together until Ed went into the service, Sam tried to lay low in the community, unlike Ed. Sam was just happy to have his land and his house and go out and fish. Sam sat on the sidelines while history was being made in Sunset Beach. He watched Ed and Odell fight and squabble over land and he saw the founders of Sea Trail decide how they were going to develop it. He's seen townspeople up in arms over bridges, sewers, cabanas, and beach parking. Sam's been around this area long enough to have seen it all.

He is well known for his huge barbeques, and I mean huge. They began in the 70s and still continue to this day. He cooks for the Highway Patrol, his friends and his family. He has a finished basement that runs the entire length of his house. It resembles a fully outfitted mess hall with long rows of tables and chairs with place settings at the ready. Off to the side is an efficient commercial kitchen. This is no fly-by-night venture. This is some serious cooking and all of it gratis. Sam has had serious health issues lately and spent several months at Duke Medical Center with heart problems, but that's not stopping him. His wife, Marie, is trying to figure out the best way to get him and his wheelchair to the lower level so he can once again host his traditional barbeques.

The Goats

Prior to the development of the Intracoastal Waterway, the barrier islands were used for grazing cattle. The local coast had many farms and even rich plantations, so livestock would have been plentiful. The cows were herded over at low tide and left to forage for the summer. Exactly how they were supplied with fresh water is not known, but artesian wells have long existed on Sunset Beach as well as on Bird Island.

In the early 60s there was an old house, supposedly an old goat herder's hut, near the North Carolina/South Carolina line that appeared as a lump in the marsh. Large herds of goats were in existence then and Schyler Stanaland had a commercial dock, informally took over as the goat herder. He took food to the spoil areas and fashioned some kind of watering arrangement.

Tommy Tucker says that the goats have been around long before anyone can place them and that he's sure they'll be here long after we're gone. The area is known as Bonaparte's Landing and is located where the sharp turn on Route 179 leads to Calabash, just past The Regency. The street leading to the water, Schyler Drive, is named after Schyler Stanaland.

Dick & Caroline Good

Dick and Caroline Good moved to Sunset Beach on December 31, 1981. They moved from suburban Pittsburgh where Dick had been a History and English teacher, then a principal for junior and senior high schools before working in administration at the superintendent level. Caroline had worked as a secretary in the Educational Psychology Department at the University of Pittsburgh. They moved to Shoreline Woods on the mainland, which at the time was in the extraterrestrial jurisdiction of Sunset Beach. They rented a home nearby while their house was being built. In April of 1982 they moved into their home and have now lived there for 28 years.

Dick says that you could say that sand dollars brought them to Sunset Beach. In 1976, they were vacationing in Myrtle Beach and Caroline saw an article about sand dollars in the local paper. The legend of the sand dollar with its biblical references intrigued her so she asked a local where she could find some. The lady recommended Sunset Beach saying, "Sand dollars are everywhere there." They drove to Sunset Beach and were delighted with their find.

Upon returning home they mentioned the sand dollar hunt and were surprised when Caroline's brother and his wife said they had just purchased land at Sunset Beach and were building an A-frame at Seaside. They visited them the following year when Sea Trail was just beginning to be developed. And of course, they kept returning. Dick and Caroline had bicycles they had received for their 25th anniversary and would ride around looking at property. If they found a lot they were interested in, they would ride to the sales office and see if it was available. One day, they found a lot on Shoreline Drive East and when they inquired about it, they were told the lot had been sold to a builder who might be willing to sell it. They arranged to buy the lot and looked for a builder among the three who were active in the area at the time. Llewellyn and Lewis built their home, as they were the only builder who provided them with a list of their specifications. Dick says they were very honorable and that he and Caroline were well pleased.

Churches were not on every corner as they are now, so when they first moved here they drove to Myrtle Beach to the Methodist Church. The church had a circuit rider at the time, so sometimes they went to Ocean Drive Presbyterian. But it was a long drive, especially during the season. When that pastor moved on, they transferred to the Ocean Drive Presbyterian Church for several years. Their neighbors, John and Marsha Warring, told them

about a Methodist church getting started locally. They encouraged Dick and Caroline to come hear their new pastor, Camille Yorkey. The Goods accompanied the Warrings to the humble little furniture store on Route 179 where the church met for services. For Dick and Caroline, it was the beginning of a long-standing church relationship that has defined their life here at Sunset Beach.

Dick says that Camille had a manner about her that was very welcoming, and that she was perhaps the most compassionate person he's ever met. When their son got sick and then died, she was wonderful, helping them get through that heart-wrenching period.

Twenty-four people started the church that is now known as Seaside United Methodist Church. The first meeting was held at the Sand Fiddler Restaurant in Southport where they met with a bishop who assigned a very young Camille Yorkey to be their pastor. That was on April 27, 1989. Their first Sunday service in the furniture store on Route 179 was on June 29, 1989. They produced their first bulletin with the fishing boat logo, now so familiar to so many, designed by Gerri Piazza, on July 2, 1989. The church was chartered by the Conference with 119 members on July 15, 1989.

The little church held an adult Sunday school class in the attic over a furniture store with Camille as the teacher for over twenty members. The Goods were so impressed with the church that they cannot now imagine having settled anywhere else. They love their church family and their community and do all they can to support both.

Dick served on the Sunset Beach Planning Board/Board of Adjustment for twelve years, from 1985-1997. He remembers that Wallace Martin was the Town Manager before he accepted the position on Bald Head Island, and that Linda Fluegel then became the new Town Manager.

Dick says that the Planning Board makes recommendations to the Council which then either supports and approves them or sends them back. He remembers two major issues the board accomplished, the sign ordinance and the zoning of Bird Island. He says they did major work on the sign ordinance and that it's the reason we don't have the proliferation of signs that so many beach communities now have. He recalls that the Council adopted their recommendation but that it was touch-and-go at the time. On the issue of Bird Island, the Price family wanted to develop it, but as we all know, that didn't quite work out.

Caroline loves books and each Tuesday morning for the past twenty years she has been a volunteer in the Rourke Library in Shallotte. She also helped to organize the church library at Seaside. For over twelve years, Dick delivered Meals-On-Wheels on Tuesday mornings while Caroline worked at the library. As this is being written, the Goods are selling their home and moving to Michigan to be with their daughter and her family. But I expect we'll see them back from time to time, visiting friends and walking along the beach . . . looking for sand dollars.

Fletcher & Kelly Frink

Fletcher and Kelly Frink owned the N.A.P.A. store in Calabash when Georgetown Road (named because it is the road leading to Georgetown, SC) was a dirt road. Fletcher (Samuel Fletcher Frink III) is native to the area and has connections to some of the most illustrious, notorious, and legendary characters in Brunswick County. He's heard it all and watched it all, and is probably the best raconteur of the area's history. His mother, Mazie, was from Ash, and until a few years ago when she died, she lived on Shoreline Drive on the Waterway. She said she hated moving from Shallotte, where she and her husband had a ranch house, accusing her husband of, "Moving her away from society."

In the 60s, when Fletcher and his parents lived in Shallotte, and later after they had moved to Ocean Isle and then to Sunset, they always had someone to help around the house. Fletcher says, "First there was Gertrude, then Mrs. Cathy; these women were black but it did not have any bearing on our family. They needed a job—we needed help. Each lady, when they worked for us, would help clean the house, do laundry, iron and cook. We loved them and I'm convinced they loved us. In the late 60s, my dad was the Master Sergeant at the National Guard Armory. He hired the first black man in the Guard in North Carolina. I was in the yard with my sisters when three men came up and dumped something in the yard. I remember my momma calling us inside, then calling the Armory for Daddy. When he got there, we saw what it was. A cross. But the men couldn't get it lit."

Fletcher tells about his uncle, S. Bunn Frink, a former district attorney and state senator. In the early 80s, Bunn's house was where Ed Gore Sr.'s house is now. Fletcher tells of the night he and Kelly went there for dinner. It was a well-known fact that every day, Monday through Saturday, Bunn went to the local ABC store and bought a fifth of whiskey. Fletcher asked him why he didn't buy something larger instead of visiting the liquor store every day and Bunn answered, "I'm going to leave a lot of money to my family but they won't get my liquor."

Eighteen years ago, in 1992, the N.A.P.A. store caught fire and even though there was a good firewall, they still had a fair amount of damage and had to sell parts out of their garage for a while. The rebuilding process took longer than it should have because the insurance company said they hadn't paid their premium. They managed to get things worked out, but it was a tough time for them. Three years later two bags of undelivered mail were seized from a postal worker's home and the insurance payment was discovered among the mail, postmarked but not delivered.

Kelly's mother, Peggy Miller, was one of the first people to buy a lot on Magnolia Drive in Seaside Station, behind the Town Hall. Kelly recalls that Paul Dennis moved her mom's trailer onto the lot for her. She adds that there were a lot of interesting characters who worked with Paul Dennis back then, including Mr. Daniels, who was known as "Skeeterman." He cleared lots at Sea Trail using a tractor and an axe, and of course, he sprayed for "skeeters."

They remember Earl Benton from Lakewood Estates, and how he used a dragline to dig out Jink's Creek to make the causeway; how Twin Lakes came into being, noting that they are man-made, not fresh water lakes; when fish was a nickel a pound or $10 a boatload, and that everyone grew up eating mullet; when beer was sold through the drive thru at a place called Jiggy's in Calabash, and that it was the coldest beer in the county. It cost you a dime more, but you could buy it even if you were only eleven; that bartering was the law of the land—no one had cash. Fletcher's parents had a hog farm, "So we always had pork chops." They would trade a hog for corn using a one-to-five ratio. His grandmother made pickles in a 50-gallon plastic trashcan and they bartered with them, too. He remembers that his mother taught people, mostly black people, to read in SENCLAND, which was what the area used to be called—SENC stood for South Eastern North Carolina.

Kelly tells about Dr. Grimmett, who still owns the gray two-story next to The Regency, and his million-dollar garden. "He had a vegetable garden across the road on land that he owned. He was offered a million dollars for the property but turned it down saying he wanted to keep his garden. When he was practicing in Loris, SC, he only charged a dollar for the delivery of a baby, so I guess he just didn't need the money."

They miss the old Magnolia Motel which was on the corner across from The Regency. Fletcher said it was a neat old L-shaped building, but was torn down when Sea Trail bought the property to make a larger, more impressive entrance for Sea Trail at Oyster Bay. At the time, Sea Trail was in a hurry trying to take advantage of a tax law that was about to change; to this date, they have not built on the property.

"Things were so different back then, especially the roads," Fletcher says. "They had paved Route 179, but they hadn't prepared the road. There was no rock bed, they just asphalted over the sand. The road was warped and had deep ruts. It was seven-feet wide with ruts so bad, well you don't even want to know what we called that road . . ." He snarls when he remembers that he got pulled over for driving on the wrong side of the road once because of the ruts. He talked to the officer for thirty minutes while he waited for the Highway Patrol to arrive and avoided a ticket because of the condition of the road. Odell agreed to prepare the road that is Angels Trace Road and Sea Trail agreed to pave it since they both used the road. But they didn't prepare it to state standards and the road had to be closed because it was so bad. Georgetown Road was just a logging road at the time, and a dirt road led to his shop. He adds that N.A.P.A. was originally known as the place next to the dumpster.

Fletcher says that it was partially because of the roads that the waterways were so popular for drug running. Southport was an hour and a half ride by car because the roads were so bad. If you had to go there—and back then it was the county seat—you had to pack a lunch. Ocean Isle had one police officer and Sunset Beach had Norman Grissett, who could usually be found sleeping in his car for lack of meaningful or interesting police work.

In the 70s and 80s, running drugs became the livelihood for many Brunswick families. He chuckles as he shakes his head. "People were so stupid thinking we couldn't tell who was doing what. The shrimp boats would come in

and the shrimp boats would go out, some with nets rotting in the riggings. There was no shrimp, yet the guys were wearing gold chains and driving El Dorados. There were drop places everywhere."

He tells about a blatant hand-off in the eighties. Fletcher was at his mother's house on the Waterway and they heard loud rumbling coming from miles away. This was before the jetties had been put in and there was only the channel. A nice yacht came into view not that far away. With his binoculars he watched as, Miami Vice-style, a briefcase was handed off and dark green bales were handed down to a speedboat that had pulled up alongside. Then the smaller, cigarette boat sped away and the beautiful yacht left, its rumble echoing down the waterway and diminishing as it left through the channel and found its way back to the ocean. "It was *absolute* daytime. It was so obvious what they were doing." Fletcher shakes his head before continuing, "There was so much money. It was too much temptation for so many. I mean here were guys making $3-$3.25 an hour instead of $200-$300 a night. Most people found it hard to turn down making in a few hours what it took months to earn." And the drug runners got even more sophisticated and ever so much bolder. He remembers the night he saw three black helicopters and a 25-foot open-hulled boat. They only went out twenty or thirty miles. "I knew what was goin' on. Everyone was catching 'square grouper,' then they were meeting at the docks at Holden. Later they would truck it off in seafood trucks."

He recalls that in '81 or '82, "The sheriff got arrested. They caught him with the goods, and so what did they do? Well, of course, they had to dispose of the contraband, so they buried it. Even though they doused the area with diesel fuel, people still came from miles around to dig it up. It was the happiest land in the world for about ninety days until they finally burned it all."

Even a small submarine was sighted running drugs. At what was once Brooks Landing, named after Joby Brooks (where the Waterway Condos are now at the end of the road between the CVS and Walgreens), there was a dock and often shrimp boats would be tied up there so they could be worked on. You had to work on them at night because it was too hot during the day. Fletcher's friend heard an odd noise and looked up in time to see a man in a small submarine pass by and wave to him.

It wasn't until the Feds decided to go undercover and not involve local law enforcement, which could tip their hand, that they were able to make any headway in curtailing the drug running. People were either involved or turned their heads to it. It would have been suicide to get between people making that kind of money, the kind that made people extremely wealthy and set them and their families up for life. With no obvious source of income, little restaurants became big restaurants; people bought property and built expensive houses, new businesses opened and expanded. The motto of the day seemed to be, "Let the good times roll."

But the Feds decided to go to war, and one night they set an ambush. Fletcher remembers that Sam Grantham was asked to go undercover. He was from Tabor City and, as he hadn't been in the area all that long, wasn't considered local. The jetties were getting ready to go in, but they weren't in yet. The bridge was the crossing point. The boats were so loaded down that they moved slowly. The Feds had guns mounted on the bows of their boats and when the drug running boats were rumbling up to the bridge the feds came out of the marshes and shot up the boats. Later, Fletcher remembers seeing what had been a nice 35-foot twin engine boat burned to the ground—no hull, just the engine and the wheelhouse remaining. Many were convicted; some went to jail—those with connections, got their hands slapped. Elections and money were exchanged for a different commodity now—forbearance.

Drugs are still a problem in Brunswick County but not the way they were back then. No one is openly referred to as "King Toot," the sounds of boats rumbling offshore late at night no longer cause law-abiding locals to cringe, and shrimp boats that go out actually come back with shrimp.

The stories that Fletcher and Kelly recall are the fabric of many lives, some spotted, some stained, some enormously funny. So if your car or truck ever breaks down, you know where to go for good service and great stories.

Clete & Betty Waldmiller

Clete Waldmiller and his wife Betty found Sunset Beach by accident. Looking for a place to spend their spring vacation in the early 80s, they requested literature from the Myrtle Beach Chamber of Commerce. Buried in the pile of brochures was a pamphlet from The Winds on Ocean Isle Beach. They made the reservation because they liked the idea of having an efficiency where they could make breakfast and lunch for their kids so they could go out for dinner at night. And the maid service was a nice break for Betty. They made The Winds their vacation spot for five or six years before they discovered Sunset Beach while driving around town. They would drive to the east end where parking was plentiful as there were no duplexes there at the time.

Clete retired in February of 1987 and they arranged to rent a house on 2nd Street while they began building their house. They bought a lot in Sea Trail long before Sea Trail was what it is today. Clete recalls Sea Trail being nothing but vacant scrub pine and oak but, regardless of its barren surroundings, they bought a lot on what would become Lakeshore Drive. Building a house on their lot didn't work out quite as planned, so the Waldmillers bought a three-year-old beach house instead. They moved in November of 1987.

A strong sense of community and the small town life were things that appealed to Clete. He regretted not being able to attend the town hall meetings, which would sometimes go until four o'clock in the morning, when he'd been a working man. His neighbor, Bill Lake, with whom he used to go fishing every day, got him interested in the Taxpayers Association. Soon after, his enthusiasm for helping the community became apparent with his idea for the "Adopt-a-Block" program. The program encouraged residents to get involved by volunteering to keep a designated area of the island clean and free of litter. Clete and Betty took on the challenge of cleaning up the causeway, which at the time was pretty filthy. It took them ten days and fifty-one garbage bags. Clete also rode his bike across the bridge to the East Entrance of Sea Trail to pick up trash that workers left behind on their lunch breaks. Clete did this for eight years, until a few restaurants other than Bill's Seafood opened and the grassy area outside the East Entrance became less popular.

Picking up litter was not the end of Clete's community involvement. He became President of the Taxpayers Association right after the dispute about the Food Lion annex. Before building (in its original location), Food Lion decided that it wanted to be annexed into the town of Sunset Beach. It was later discovered that Food Lion only wanted this because they wanted a beer and wine license. Brunswick County at that time was dry. After some finagling with numbers and taxes, the shopping center proposal went through, mostly because of a proposed future occupancy tax on condos yet to be built. This caused rifts between board members, President Mason Barber, the Taxpayers Association, and the townspeople. A year or two after the debacle, Clete became president. Although he no longer had disputes with Mason, he had other challenges on the horizon, most concerning the issue of the new bridge.

Charles & Aileen Smith

Charles Lindbergh Smith and his wife, Aileen, came to this area from Fayetteville, where they lived for forty years. Charlie worked at Ft. Bragg for twenty-eight years before taking an "early out" in 1988. Aileen was a nurse at Cape Fear Valley Medical in Fayetteville where she was a supervisor for 35 years. She credits her career to the local Rotary Club and their $100 scholarship which started her on the three-year nursing program. She worked while attending school and often studied nine to ten hours at night to take an 8 A.M. exam. She was paid $20 to $30 a month. Their first trip to Sunset Beach was in 1958. Charlie says there were twelve cottages on the island, all on the ocean. He said Mannon Gore was the "Entrepreneur" who designed and built the swing bridge. Mannon was fond of telling people that, "If you were on the island after midnight, you were on the island 'til morning."

Charlie and his dad bought a lot at 502 East Main Street in 1958 and built a house on it in 1959. It was a summerhouse at first, the lumber, knotty pine, as Charlie remembers, was purchased and brought from the Sandhills area of North Carolina. Vester Wallace was their carpenter, and when Vester came to work he had to come prepared to spend the day as there was nothing on the island then, no place to get food or anything to drink.

Charlie became in the 60s, and he boat commercially. caught were cleaned road from his house their fish heads on Captain Charlie began to charter his The fish that were on the lot across the and everyone threw a mound they called "Charlie's Place." It was a time when anyone could walk about on Bird Island in the nude if they wanted to. Not saying they did mind you, but they could have had they been so inclined.

The Smiths had three children, Ron, Linn (short for Lindbergh), and Tammy, the youngest. Years later, there were seven grandchildren and together they vacationed at the Smith Family Vacation House until it was torn down in 1990. A new one was built, this one with whitewashed, pickled wainscoting—but more on the new house later.

Aileen remembers the first house a little less fondly than Charlie. She says anything they needed they had to bring and that included the food as well as all the water they planned on using—and the ice. She'd pack for days to get ready for their vacations. And it was hot, very hot. There were no fans, no air conditioning, and, in the beginning, no shower. The boys liked to jump in the sand dunes so that was a huge problem. "And the kitchen, my gosh was it hot!" The guys would catch fish and expect her to cook it for dinner. That meant frying, standing over the heat of a stove in a sweltering hot kitchen, cooking for as many as twenty at times. Any woman over the age of forty knows this was no vacation for the lady of the house. Back in Fayetteville, everything then had to be put away.

Eventually a combination post office and grocery store opened where the Waves store is now. Niven Milligan and his wife, Frances, owned it. They remember when Ronnie and Clarice Holden opened Twin Lakes Restaurant. Ronnie cooked and Clarice was both the hostess and the waitress. Until then the Smiths had never dined out when vacationing at the beach. What a treat for Aileen!

Charlie says there was a water issue at first. In 1959 the tide line came up to the bottom of their steps. Then the primary dune built itself up to twenty-three feet and obscured the view of the ocean. Everyone had to put in their own well, so Charlie chose the opposite side of the lot, where there was a seawall, and dug seventeen feet into the dune. He says the "the purest water as it the sand. Then much came and brought came because there systems failing. You that water."  island water was, was filtered through later the County water. County water were so many septic didn't want to drink

Until they decided old house withstood to tear it down, the hurricanes and storms, storms not categorized but often worse than hurricanes. The worst they'd had happen over the years was a few shutters breaking loose. They lived with Mother Nature, opening the doors and letting the wind blow through, until it was time to modernize and build a new house. I'm fairly certain Aileen had something to do with that decision. The Smiths bought a lot on 6th Street and Canal from a couple who was divorcing, planning to build the house they would retire in. Bill Hunt did the contracting and they began building in 1982.

Charlie's dad had originally bought a lot on each side of their house, saying if he could find someone to double his money he'd take it. One lot lasted a year and he was paid $5,000 for it. He thought he'd made a pretty good deal, until three years later, he got $15,000 for the other one.

Charlie says that a handshake was all you needed to make a deal with Mannon Gore. Then one day Mannon had a heart attack and his son, Ed, was left to run the motor grader and keep the roads clear (a constant battle as the sand always needed to be pushed off the road). Shortly after, Mannon left for Emerald Isle and then Florida. With the proceeds from the sale of his development company, which he sold to Ed and Dinah, Mannon went into real estate in Florida, and according to Charlie, made millions.

He recalls that Bill and Minnie Hunt's house, referred to as *The Hunt Club*, was two doors down. Minnie and her first husband, Bill Whaley, had originally built the *Star Thrower*. When Bill and Minnie sold the lot, *The Hunt Club* was moved. Their next house was a passive solar house designed so that the southern exposure could heat the home during the winter months. Charlie says the winters didn't seem so harsh back then. He remembers sitting on his porch in December in short-sleeved shirts. Charlie says September was the time to blow out the pipes and shut down for the winter. This was before the season got extended. For some, the season continues through the holidays now.

Charlie's mother and father had an efficiency apartment under the house and lived there permanently from the late sixties until 1971, when his dad died after walking his dog. His mother lived with them for many years before she died in the 80s. With fondness, Charlie remembers coming down on Friday nights with their boat, a Hawkeye III Diesel, that brings a twinkle to his eye (he previously owned a Hawkeye I and a Hawkeye II—a 17-footer and a 22-footer). I'm told it could do 25 miles at 18 knots in an hour and a half. He would catch black sea bass and king fish for a big fish fry. He and his friends often enjoyed all-night or late-night poker parties after a day of fishing. He hosted a few Colonels and even a General once. One time he almost broke down off Holden Beach with ten or twelve people on board. He refers to it as "The Iced Tea Incident." At the time the County was "dry," but at certain establishments, if you asked for the "good" iced tea, you might get something other than steeped orange pekoe leaves. He and his guests were dining and unbeknownst to Charlie, one of the guests asked if they had good iced tea. The waitress said, "Yes" and proceeded to fill their glasses with whiskey—quite a few times. But despite their inebriated state, his guests were bound and determined they were going fishing. They were twenty-two miles out when they broke down with six-foot seas coming in and everyone got seasick. Charlie managed to get the boat restarted and got everyone in safely.

In 1993 Aileen told Charlie she didn't like the hassles of living on the beach anymore. She worried about the bridge

with regard to emergencies so they decided to move off the island and built a house on Horsebranch Road on the mainland at Ocean Isle Beach. The beach house became available for rent that year. Now it is rented almost all year long so Charlie never needs to winterize it anymore. He says that people are realizing that the nicest time to come down is in October, November and December. He has a lot of repeat renters who set aside the same time every year and reserve it before leaving to head back home. He also lets his grandkids block out the time that they want to use it.

Charlie remembers in vivid detail the time the Sunset Beach Bridge was hit by a barge putting it out of commission for ten days. "The barge was going south loaded with dredge pipes. He was on the landside and the pipes were stacked higher than the wheelhouse. The Captain was trying to compensate for the wind and miscalculated. He took out sixty-feet of the bridge and went over it as if it was made of toothpicks. They stopped him at the South Carolina line because he couldn't stop. They needed LST's (boats) to get people on and off the island. It took ten days to repair the damage as they had to reset the poles."

And then in March of 1993, there was a horrible storm with 80-90 mph winds. They tied the bridge up with only five minutes notice. The temperature dropped to freezing and snow was blowing horizontally. Charlie had gone to check on the house and got caught over there along with the people working on the island, who had to stay in their vehicles. At the time, the electric wires were overhead so the Town shut off the power for safety reasons. A downed line blowing around could electrocute someone or start a fire. Charlie made it to the house just as the power died and he had to bundle himself on the couch with all the blankets he could manage to find just to stay warm.

He hoped to live long enough to cross the new bridge but he didn't know if he would or not as, "The darned thing just keeps getting delayed." (At the time of this interview the new bridge had not yet been started. The Sunset Beach Tax Payers had made their final appeal and a decision had not yet been determined; it was overturned a few months later. Unfortunately, Charlie will not get see the "darned thing" completed as he died last year).

Raymond & Miriam Marks

Raymond and Miriam Marks lived in Rockingham, NC. One day, as a lark, Raymond rode with a friend who was a real estate agent to a place called Sunset Beach. He had always taken his family to Ocean Drive in North Myrtle Beach for vacations and had never even heard of Sunset Beach. Much to his wife's chagrin, he came home with a beach house.

In 1967, the little "beach shack," as Miriam so fondly referred to it, on an oceanfront lot, took $10,000 out of their savings. At the time, it was the last house on the east end of the island. It was also the last lot on the east end. There are now about thirty lots where before there was only a channel.

Raymond told his wife, "I think we can fix it up." When she first saw the house, her heart fell to her shoes. *What had he done with their money?* She thought for sure that he had squandered it. The house was called *Boyd's Nest* and some prominent people in Hamlet had owned it before them.

They tossed out all the old furniture and began to set the house to rights. Structurally, it was pretty sound with nice pine hardwood floors and pine paneling on the walls. There was an odd seam down the middle of the floor though, as if it had once been two parts. Sound familiar? (See Hugh Munday's profile. In 1994 this house, originally military housing at Fort Bragg, was moved and Hugh bought it).

The Marks had a huge tidal pond between them and the ocean for many years; in fact, they had a hard time getting to the ocean, as they had to go around it. The pond was so large that people often came to fish in it. For many years they knew no one, as there were only about fifteen houses on the island. Miriam recalls that, "It was deserted, like a piece of paradise. It was beautiful, like heaven. But it was the end of the world." The only people they saw were the drivers and Mannon who was operating the dredge. For two years they endured the steady humdrum of the dredge as Mannon worked to fill in the land. In those days developers could do things on the coast that would be difficult if not impossible to do now with the Coastal Area Management Authority restrictions. But dredging didn't involve very much red tape back then. By 1969 Mannon had just about finished his ambitious reclamation project, dredging the throat of Tubbs Inlet between the end of Sunset Beach and the beginning of Ocean Isle Beach. He had added enough sand to the beach to provide the foundation for more than thirty additional houses.

The process was not without its pitfalls however; many times the Marks family thought their little beach house was going to wash away. There was often water under it as if it were floating. During one astronomical (lunar) high tide, the water was so high that Raymond called Mannon over and asked him what he planned to do about it. They were sure they were going to lose their house. Mannon assured them that if they did, if it truly washed away, he would provide them with a new lot and put a house on it for them. Two or three days later, the inlet was blown out (see Edward Gore, Jr. and Ronnie Holden) and it wasn't ever a problem again. Even the pond, that had been more of a nuisance than anything, was no longer an issue as it dried up. Soon the beach in front of them began to grow until they had the length of several football fields in front of them.

Years after the inlet had stabilized and the sand had accreted so much that they had hundreds of feet of sand between them and the ocean, there was talk about Ed's development company putting in another row of houses in front of theirs. For some people this couldn't happen as their lots were deeded down to the ocean, but for the Marks and many others, their lots were only deeded to what at the time had been the high water line, a mere thirty feet or so from their house. It was entirely possible that other houses could be built in front of theirs, even another road put in, and that they would no longer have the view they had come to love, or direct access to the ocean. And of course, their property value would plummet, since they would no longer be oceanfront. There was a lot of anxious debate, but talk of usurping that land eventually died out.

Miriam remembers there was a telephone pole with a box about twenty feet from their house and when it went down there was only one other phone in the area, and that was at the grocery store (where the Wings store is now). The grocery store, run by Nivan and Frances Milligan, had a phone booth. If someone called, Mr. Milligan would get in his car, drive over the bridge, and relay the message.

She remembers the only neighbors on the block at the time were Dr. Al Wells and his wife Margaret, from Laurinburg. They built a house called *Seascape* and came often with their two little boys. They had two sailboats that the boys would go out in. Dr. Wells also bought the lot where *Beach Music* is today. He bought the extra lot in case their original lot washed away. The original *Seascape* was torn down two years ago and a more modern house was built. The Goodmans bought the first lot after Mannon and Ed filled in the land east of the Marks' house. Miriam's only regret now is that when they had the opportunity, Raymond didn't follow through with his plans to buy one of the lots as an investment. Al Morrison built the house for the Goodmans and years later, Raymond and Miriam thought about selling their house and purchasing it because it was such a fine house, but they didn't.

In 1994, Raymond and Miriam gave *Boyd's Nest* to Hugh Munday in return for him moving it. Today, Miriam lives in the home they built called *Plum Nelly*. It is called *Plum Nelly* because Raymond, as the Mayor of Rockingham, had to name the road they had built their house on back home and he had named the road Plum Nelly as it was, "Plum in the county," and, "Nelly (nearly) in town." So when it was time to name the beach house, it became *Plum Nelly* also, because it was, "Plum in the water," and, "Nelly in the ground."

Miriam is now in her nineties and while dealing with fading eyesight, her mind is as sharp as ever. She tells about the yearly Christmas parties Minnie and Bill Hunt had where Minnie gave out hand-made calendars with memorabilia of the old days as monthly pictures. She remembers the wonderful picnics—the Annual Mad Inlet Labor Day Picnics where Frank Nesmith would be the Mayor of the Picnic, and Bill Hunt would be the Sheriff of the Picnic—grills were set up for cooking and a photo album from the previous year's event made the rounds. You were instructed to bring your own food and drink, ants, guitars, ukes, photos to share, and a smile. Can you imagine—they cooked on the beach—with a grill!

Ginny Lassiter

Ginny and her son, Scott (Summerfield), moved to Sunset Beach in 1978. She rented a cottage across from Frank Nesmith for a while, and then moved to 27th Street on the island near Joe and Leola Spivey.

She remembers watching the fishermen setting out their nets to catch mullet and bringing in huge catches with the use of a tractor, as the nets were too heavy to haul them in by hand—this was mostly done to the right of the pier. People used to eat smoked mullet. Often locals would put them on a stick, poke the sticks in the sand and cook them over red hot briquettes. This would allow the greasy oil from the fish to leak out, flame up, and make them crisp. This was in the late 70s and early 80s. It's rare that you can find a place that sells mullet these days, but it was a staple back then.

Walking to Bird Island necessitated a keen awareness of the tides. It was so easy to get over there and get lost in the peacefulness and then be unable to return when the high tide came in. It was a very slow lifestyle compared to today.

Ginny says that at one point, before they replaced the barge part of the bridge and before there were stoplights for it, two cars could actually pass each other at the same time, if they were careful. She said it was a game of chicken that the locals often played.

Ginny and her second husband, Joe Temple, sold their house to friends and moved to an area on the island known as "The Old Campground," at 19th and Northshore Drive (it once belonged to Jim and Jacquelyn Bowen). You reached it by taking Cobia and then driving east to the back of the island. She says it was a very isolated, but safe place and she never worried about her young son. They had jon boats and little sailboats, paddle boats and all manner of fishing gear. Name anything water related and they owned it, including a golden retriever. This was before leash laws so the dog was able to come and go as he pleased. Scott even had friends on the island, Tommy Tucker's children, although older, and Gail and David Keaton's son Matthew. Amy and Joel Edge had a son but they moved away fairly early on. Scott had plenty of friends and played well by himself. He was much younger than the Gore children, about ten years younger than Greg Gore. The school bus came all the way around to their street, which she says was a blessing.

The closest regular grocery store was the I.G.A. at Ocean Isle Beach. There were two stores in Shallotte, Hill's and Wilson's, but that was twelve miles away. Twelve miles in the other direction was an A & P in North Myrtle Beach. There were no grocery stores in Little River that she can recall.

Where Bill's Seafood is now, there was a small town convenience store called Hardees, run by Paul and Geneva Hardee. They sold seafood and basic things like bread, milk, and beer. You could even charge things to your account. They just wrote your name in a book along with the amount owed. They didn't have liquor by the drink at that time and Ginny remembers that at the Bridgeside Restaurant, you could take your own bottle in with you. It was the same at the Twin Lakes Restaurant across the road. You asked for the mixer and poured in your own alcohol. A few years later, The Bridgeside closed and Art Rotundo leased the space and opened the Italian Fisherman.

The winters were desolate, but Ginny, very much the creative type and an avid reader, liked her solitude and never ran out of things to do. "But," she says, "you had to *go* somewhere to buy *anything*. There was no Wal-mart, no Belk, no grocery stores." She remembers a lady named Anne Beckham, saying she was a real free spirit with a flower-child personality who opened a small restaurant and made great gourmet meals. But she was probably twenty years ahead of her time, and even though she made fabulous gourmet dinners, she couldn't make a go of it. There just were not enough people who would buy them. Her permit was for take out only. Ginny adds that, "It's the kind of place that would go over well now, but at the time it just wasn't what the people in the area wanted."

Ginny and her husband's business, Kool-a-brew Inc., started on the island. When it outgrew the space, they moved the manufacturing business to Calabash to Koolabrew Drive where it still is today.

Ginny says the hardest years were 1984-1987. The winters were harsh but she still bundled up and managed to walk on the beach. Her husband had cancer and was very sick so there was a lot of traveling for treatment. When the barge hit the bridge and knocked it out of commission for over a week, it was very hard to manage everything, but they did. The town rigged up a barge that a boat towed back and forth so people could get on and off the island. She remembers they had to climb up and down a ladder to get on and off it and that was hard for her husband to manage. But, she remembers with a smile, they got the school bus onto the makeshift ferry so the driver could collect the school kids and then bring them back. Ginny's husband died in 1986.

December of 1988 and January of 1989 they experienced an astronomical lunar high tide that flooded the area. The whole end of the island in front of her house was covered with water. All of Northshore and part of Cobia were underwater. At the time her house was on a point with nothing in front of it (she says the houses that are there really shouldn't be there now). Ginny was supposed to be at a tradeshow in Myrtle Beach that morning. Her son was at his grandparents, so she was the only one at home. Dutifully, she got ready and ventured out. She got to Northshore and Cobia before the water was so deep it flooded in under the car's doors. She remembers she was wearing hose and a dress, and it was cold when she had to get out and wade back to the house. There wasn't anyone else to work the booth at the show so she called an employee who brought a truck to drive her there. The same thing happened a month later. It was like her house was on its own island. It was unnerving, realizing how fast Mother Nature could overtake man-made boundaries. When the developers started talking about building more houses in that area, she said, "Oh no, please don't do that!" But they did anyway. And what was once a bird sanctuary, with a panoramic view three quarters of the way around to the marshes, the Intracoastal, and to the ocean beyond, was gone. She says it was a phenomenal view. The sun came up in the east and was so beautiful to watch. She says she would probably never have sold her house if they hadn't built those houses there, but with the magnificent view gone, she couldn't stay. It could never be like it was—the way she and her son would always remember it. They couldn't do the things that they used to do—the boating, the fishing, and the leisurely walks along the point as the sun came up. So she moved to a house on the Waterway at Ocean Isle Beach. After renting the beach house for a few years, she sold it. She can see it, along with all the others that now surround it, from her deck on the Waterway.

She said it was a different way of life back then. There were a lot of free spirits and people who had run away from a hectic life in the big city. One such lady was Claudia Sailor, Frank Nesmith's girlfriend at the time. She taught art in Fayetteville and kept a jon boat on Ginny's property. She gave Ginny's son, Scott, a couple of her drawings. Ginny says she was an interesting person. If you've read this book carefully, you may have gleaned something here. Do the initials K.S. mean anything to you?

Another free spirit was Joan who owned a dress shop called The Beach Quarter. Ginny says she couldn't be a nine-to-fiver even to make things work out. She had to be a little different, so the business had to close.

Ginny has seen a lot of changes since coming to Sunset Beach. She and her third husband own the Sunset River Marketplace Gallery on Beach Road just before Route 179 meets Highway 17 at the southern end of Calabash. If you doubt her love of the area and beaches in general, go see the coastal art on display there; some of the best artists on the East Coast are represented. Ginny and her husband generously host many benefits for local charities and sponsor workshops and lectures for local authors and artists. This book, for instance, can be purchased there!

At the top is the present day Town Hall. Below is the old Town Hall. It was on Shoreline Drive.

Did You Know?

Bill's Seafood used to be Sunset Seafood and Sam B. Somersett was the owner.

Twin Lakes Grocery was located where the Waves store is now. Nivan and Frances Milligan ran it. They had a complete line of groceries, magazines, fishing tackle and bait. They were agents for N.C. Hunting and Fishing licenses, sold novelties and souvenirs, rented TVs and even beach cottages. The store was also the island grill, the first post office, and they even delivered phone messages to the island.

There was a Sunset Strip Motel.

The Vesta Pier was a member of the Southeastern N.C. Beach Association Fishing Rodeo.

The original realty sales office, which belonged to the Gores, was accidentally demolished when the wrecking company destroyed the wrong building.

The Vesta Pier was built over the *Vesta*. The boiler of the *Vesta*, a blockade runner, can be seen just above the water in the center of this picture.

Mannon Gore gave away a free 17-foot boat at the land auctions and there were 1,148 lots to choose from. The original financing terms offered were 29% down with the balance due in two to five years.

Homeowners on the island had a big Annual Labor Day picnic at Mad Inlet every year and a "crying in" at the pier to say good-bye to summer. Just after Christmastime each year, there was a "Three-Scotch House Count". A group of islanders took a bottle of scotch and drove around the island noting each new house and the street it was on. It usually took three scotches to accomplish the task, hence the name.

The wheelhouse on the original bridge was on the left side when facing the island.

Mannon Gore purchased Sunset Beach for $55,800.

Wallace Martin, the first Town Administrator, was also the building inspector and helped operate the water system. Before that, he was Vice President of Finance and head of the accounting and statistics department for Pfeiffer College, where he also taught business. He was a heavyweight boxer at the U.S. Naval Academy, graduated from Western Carolina University, and earned a master's degree at Appalachian State. Martin was also a college and high school football coach, a high school principal, and a state legislator.

The breakthrough for Tubbs Inlet occurred on or about April 21, 1970. Odell Williamson said the inlet was created by the dredging done by the developers of Sunset Beach, accusing both Mannon and Ed Gore for the loss of land by erosion to Ocean Isle Beach saying, "It was a land grab." Ed Gore advocated stabilization of both Tubbs and Mad Inlets. The Army Corps of Engineers in Wilmington and the Conservation and Development Department in Raleigh agreed that the proposed plans were reasonable. The estimated cost in 1971 was $250,000-$280,000. The Little River Inlet jetties (both east and west) were installed ten years later. The project began in 1980 and was finished in 1983.

The N.C. League of Municipalities recognized the Town of Sunset Beach for collecting 99 percent of the property taxes due. This was an annual award, and the town claimed the record for five straight years. The outstanding record was attributable to Linda Fluegel, who was Town Clerk at the time.

In 1972, a Charlotte-based construction firm, Carolina Caribbean, planned a $15,000,000 recreational resort in Calabash, including a golf course, tennis courts, a marina, single-family homes, and condos.

The most bizarre news story of 1970 was that, according to the State ABC Board, the Sunset Beach liquor store was losing money. No one could figure out how that was happening. There was no competition, the merchandise wasn't obsolete, and there were no unfair labor practices or strikes. It was baffling news to be sure; it was likened to the only undertaker in Dodge City going broke during the pinnacle of shootouts. Were they allowing people to run a tab?

Whenever a sign was posted for a bridge closing for maintenance, the notice often included this advice: Drivers are encouraged to find an alternate route.

There once was a sign between Sunset Beach and Bird Island that read: Entering Sunset Beach—No Nudity Allowed.

Rolfe Neill, publisher of the Charlotte Observer, called Ocean Isle and Sunset Beaches, "The last two oceanfront pearls." (August 22, 1982).

The Sunset Beach Motel was demolished in February, 2006.

During the summer of 1982, the Kindred Spirit mailbox was orange and actually had a post office address: Kindred Spirit, Rte 1 Isle De Claudia, Sunset Beach 28459. Could this be why it is assumed the Kindred Spirit is a woman? (If this were a treasure hunt, I would tell you to go to Ginny Lassiter's profile).Note the zip code, which is now a zip code for Shallotte.

In the 80s, a former Sunset Beach Chief of Police went to jail for dealing in stolen goods. So did the County Sheriff, for helping to transport illegal drugs.

The Environmental Impact Statement completed in October 1997 is almost three inches thick.

The unique east-to-west orientation of Sunset Beach not only protects it from erosion, but also allows for exceptionally beautiful sunrises and sunsets over the water. Sunset Beach is an accreting beach, one of the few on the east coast.

Calabash Presbyterian Church is now in Sunset Beach.

Bird Island is a 1,300-acre State preserve and home to over 20 species of birds. It is aptly named. The Purple Sandpiper is found exclusively on Bird Island. Look for it at the jetty just past the NC/SC state line.

Sunset Beach has been called "The most beautiful three miles of coastline in North Carolina." It is the smallest of the three barrier islands that make up the South Brunswick Islands. It is the nesting ground for endangered Loggerhead sea turtles and home to much beloved wood storks.

The Sunset Beach Turtle Watch Program is a private nonprofit program of volunteers who help monitor, record and protect nesting sites. Harassment of sea turtles or their nests is a violation of State and Federal laws and punishable by fines up to $100,000 and/or imprisonment.

The Brooks family owned land at Sunset Beach dating back to Civil War times.

Ocean Harbor was once an island. It was called Corkin's Neck. The lakes there now were inlets from the sea.

Quote attributed to a homeowner at Bonaparte's Landing during Hurricane Hazel on October 15, 1954, "When the water came over the island, I left." Must have been a scary sight.

Great Grandfather Stanaland had nine children. He brought in a tutor who, unbeknownst to him had Tuberculosis, and almost wiped out the whole family (some say it was Typhoid Fever).

Before the roads were paved, most long distance travel was by boat. If you wanted to go to Wilmington, you left from Pea Landing in Calabash.

Georgetown Road was originally called the Sea Trail as it was the trail to the sea.

Up until the 50s, money was not a commodity. It was a primarily an agrarian culture. This area was the poorest section of the county. If someone died they were buried in a plot out back. Family and church were the way of life. People hunted, fished, and crabbed as the seasons allowed. If they needed money, they hired out as carpenters or bricklayers.

In 1963, when Sunset Beach was incorporated, there were 30 residents. Of the 30, 29 voted, 8 ran, and 6 were elected. Mannon Gore was the first mayor. In 1972, nine years later, there were only 72 people living in Sunset Beach. The boom hit in the later part of the 80s.

In 1963 an oceanfront lot cost $1,000; in 1965 it was $5,000; in 1967 it was $10,000. Now an ocean front lot is valued from $750,000 to $3,000,000.

Although the canals had been worked on since the American Revolution, the construction of the Atlantic Intracoastal Waterway by the U.S. Army Corps of Engineers was not authorized by the United States Congress until 1919. It was not a navigable route for boats here until the mid-1930s.

After Odell Williamson saw the success of Larry Young's golf course venture, he built a few of his own courses. It's said that when the first one was finished, he stood on the backside and announced, "That's Oyster Bay. This is the Pearl."

Sunset Beach was first listed in the Rand McNally Road Atlas in 1989. At the time, the town had a permanent population of 629 residents and 7,200 seasonal residents.

Sunset Beach has had more female mayors than male mayors.

The permanent population of Sunset Beach is now approximately 3,300.

The original charter with the State General Assembly that incorporated Sunset Beach as a town was House Bill Number 118, Chapter 93.

There are three Sunset Beach churches and services on the island.

Looking Back

The Sunset Beach Bridge

When narrowing down the choices for the most iconic symbol for Sunset Beach, you'd be hard-pressed to find someone to argue against the quaint, fifty-two-year-old swing bridge having that honor. But, over the years, *arguing* about the bridge has become a way of life for many people.

How does one pare down a twenty-five-year-old battle to two pages? When the idea of a high-span bridge was first proposed, The Sunset Beach Taxpayers Association (S.B.T.A.) believed that if you build it, they will come. The Town of Sunset Beach believed if you didn't build it, bad things could happen to people on the island. The North Carolina DOT, as the benefactor in charge, believed it was time to grow up, literally—65 feet up. Wow, I did it in one paragraph!

The Sunset Beach Taxpayers Association, along with its attorneys, used the legal system to their advantage. They had a great strategy and used every environmental concern to its utmost advantage, and were able to stall the inevitable much longer than they probably ever thought they would. They had a sacred mission and they were dedicated to it. They wanted to preserve the island for future generations; they wanted to keep the commercial aspects that befall popular beaches to a minimum; and, ultimately, they did not want the changes that a new bridge would bring—more traffic, more crime, more people to sully the island, and more tourists to ignore the rules. These were honorable and forward thinking concepts that were often misconstrued as selfishly motivated attempts to keep the island all to themselves.

The anonymity of many of the Association members was a result of the tension and the hard feelings that developed as people took sides on this controversial issue. The most outspoken were, of course, well known. Unofficially, it was believed the supporters numbered in the hundreds—comprised of islanders, part-time owners, and loyal vacationers. The reality was that the number of supporters was far less. Many joined initially and then dropped out when they realized it wasn't simply a group of islanders who paid taxes and wanted a voice. Others dropped out of the fold when they realized the scope of involvement required and how it could affect relationships within the community. But the ones who remained were a stalwart group and ready to get to work. Fliers were printed, t-shirts were sold, and world-class attorneys were put on retainer. The battle was on. Despite years of meetings where heated discussions were the norm, no one would budge. The NC DOT became a major player when it wrested the decision from the opposing factions and decided to stop repairing the old bridge. They insisted it be replaced. And like a parent laying down the law, they held firm.

The big guns came out. Challenges were made based on the environment. Serious issues were raised that the State could not ignore. An environmental impact study was ordered, one that took far longer than anyone had anticipated and cost hundreds of thousands of dollars.

When the study was finally released (ten years later), finding in favor of the Town of Sunset Beach and the NC DOT, appeals kept the matter unresolved for eight more years.

Meanwhile, the old bridge was having serious maintenance issues. Breakdowns were becoming more frequent, often stranding both homeowners and vacationers for days at a time. The Town of Sunset Beach was concerned for the safety of both the residents and the tourists. There were times when extreme conditions, occurring at high or low tides during lunar cycles, made it impossible for rescue equipment to cross over to the island. Someone on the island needing medical help could not get it in a timely fashion; a fire burning out of control could have free reign as winds blew cinders from one house to another; the whole island could be lost. During peak times in the summer, the police had their hands full dealing with miles of backed-up traffic. When swimmers on the island got caught in rip tides, the response time for a rescue boat depended more on the status of the bridge than anything else. Something had to give.

NC DOT gave the Town two options—a 35-foot-high drawbridge and a 65-foot-high span bridge. Surveys were sent out, meetings had standing room only, and tempers were riding high as the inevitability of a new bridge was realized. But the SBTA won yet another appeal—long enough to stall the project and cause the cost of a new bridge to soar. When the same judge who had heard the first complaints and issued the impact study, Judge Earl Britt, denied the appeal after two years, the offer to bid went out. Even after English Construction was awarded the contract for $32 million, there was still unease that a last minute legal maneuver would delay the ground breaking. One was tried, but did not succeed. During the first week of March in 2008, work began. Trees were cut down, lots were cleared and equipment began arriving. The three-year project was underway. As you are reading this, the new bridge is in place, dedicated to coincide with the 2010 Sunset at Sunset Festival and the publication of *Sunset* *Beach: A History.*

What follows is a some of the headlines or cheers, depending on you were on. But first a timeline of events and that caused either groans which side of the "Bridge" little bridge history:

The first bridge to of Sunset Beach was developer Mannon C. drawbridge controlled by was replaced by the North Transportation in 1961 cross over to the island finished in 1958 by local Gore. It was a cable swing a three-drum winch. It Carolina Department of and then again in 1973.

The maintenance crews from Wilmington replaced it a fourth time in 1984 and now it stands in all its glory—all 508 feet 6 inches of it. A lot of repairs have been made over the years (costing an average of $500,000-$750,000 a year) and it was past time for a new one long ago. Toreutic worms have eaten the wood, boring holes everywhere, riddling it and infesting every plank. The pontoons keeping it afloat are leaking, and it has an amazing propensity for breaking down on holiday weekends. In 2007, the bridge was inspected and rated by the NC DOT. It received one of the lowest ratings ever given, a five on a scale of 100. It's quaint, it's photogenic, and now it's literally . . . history.

Sunset Beach Bridge—A Timeline

1958
Sunset Beach founder and visionary, Mannon C. Gore builds the cable swing bridge connecting the mainland to the island.
1961
A one-lane wooden-decked bridge on pontoons is erected.
1973
The bridge is essentially rebuilt with the same key components by NC DOT.
1983
Both Ocean Isle and Holden Beach residents anticipate their new high-rise bridges, approved by their towns,

while NC DOT deals with the delays for a new Sunset Beach bridge due to opposition from residents.

1984

Sunset Beach property owners favor keeping the barge-style bridge, much to the chagrin of developers who insist there is a need for a high-rise structure.

1984

The bridge is rebuilt, again. This will be the final time. From here on, it's patch, patch, patch.

1986

Ocean Isle gets its bridge ($8.6 million) and Holden Beach's is dedicated. Holden Beach received the bridge that had ben planned for Sunset Beach and it only cost them $4.1 million. The NC DOT budget for the proposed bridge at Sunset Beach is $5.2 million. Right-of-way acquisitions are scheduled. For the fiscal year 1979-1980, NC DOT spent $913,075 repairing the bridge. They figured it was only going to get worse. For the money spent maintaining the bridge, they could have built a new one years ago. They become adamant about replacing it.

1989

The Sunset Beach Taxpayers Association steps up opposition beginning a "Save our Bridge" campaign on Labor Day Weekend. Renowned marine biologist Orrin Pilkey is guest speaker at the rally.

1990

Town leaders lobby for construction of a high-rise bridge (now estimated at $11.1 million). SBTA continues to block replacement and files a lawsuit to preserve the bridge. Judge Earl Britt cancels all permits and rules in favor of the SBTA and orders a thorough environmental impact study.

1995

Although not yet signed off on (finally approved in 1997), the environmental study group concludes a new bridge won't, "Measurably contribute to cumulative impacts to the human or natural environment on the island."

1996

NC DOT endorses construction of a 65-foot tall span saying it is the preferred replacement for the one-lane swing bridge and projects completion before 2000.

1998

The SBTA approaches NC DOT and requests they replace the existing bridge with another pontoon bridge suggesting they charge a toll for people to visit the island. Their second choice is a 16-foot high center/corridor bascule bridge, also a drawbridge to collect a toll.

1999

State transportation secretary David McCoy endorses an $18.2 million high-rise bridge for the island for unimpeded traffic flow and public safety.

2000

A federal judge lifts the injunction that delayed replacement of the bridge for ten years. NC DOT earmarks $500,000 for final right-of-way acquisition in 2002 (they had already secured some property toward this end), and $5 million is approved for construction over the next three years. An attorney for the SBTA says the group will challenge the Environmental Impact Statement. NC DOT describes the 40-year-old bridge as structurally deficient and functionally obsolete. SBTA tries another tack by saying improved traffic flow would spoil the quiet lifestyle of the island residents and alludes to a surge in crime.

2002

NC DOT holds a public meeting at the Sea Trail Conference Center. It is very well attended. Their stance is, "Not if a bridge will be built after nearly a quarter-century of delays, but what kind." SBTA follows through with litigation filed in Federal Court in Wilmington.

2003

SBTA has stalled bridge construction for nearly 25 years. NC DOT makes plans to break ground within 18-24 months.

2004

U.S. District Judge Malcolm Howard issues a memorandum mandating NC DOT meet procedural requirements for performing an environmental impact study for a new bridge clearing the way for construction to begin. Due to design delays, the new high-rise bridge won't be completed until the end of 2008.

2005

A triumvirate of Sunset Beach council candidates, (Richard Cerrato, Warren Kuhler, and Richard Marchell) jumps on the bandwagon and denounces the future high-rise at a November election debate.

2006

State revenues take a nosedive but construction of the $18.3 million high-rise bridge is on target to begin the following year (according to NC DOT division engineer Allen Pope).

2007

A third party appeal by SBTA and the Brunswick Environmental Action Team (BEAT) to deny a construction permit for the high-rise bridge—due to concerns about storm water runoff and other environmental issues—is denied by Courtney Hackney, chairman of the Coastal Resources Commission, on grounds that it's frivolous.

2007

The Town of Sunset Beach urges NC DOT to approve the latest $31.9 million bid. SBTA and BEAT file an 11th-hour motion for an injunction to stop NC DOT from proceeding. Bids have to go out twice because they differ so greatly from NC DOT's estimates. English Construction from Lynchburg, Virginia is awarded the contract.

2008

Construction of the new high-rise bridge begins. It is slated to be completed in December, 2010

2010

The new bridge is dedicated on October 1, 2010.

Newspaper and magazine headlines from *The Brunswick Beacon, The Wilmington Star News, USA Today, South Brunswick Magazine,* **and** *Our State:*

The Little Bridge that Could
Pin Slips Rendering Bridge Useless to Boats
Bridge Breakdown Isolates Island
One Person Finds Bright Spot in Bridge Closure (she got a free boat ride from boaters ferrying people)
New Bridge Four Years from Completion
Once Again, Sunset Beach Bridge Out of Service (Labor Day Weekend)
Sunset Beach Bridge Closes Following Damage by Boats
Sunset Beach Bridge Damaged
Bridge Hurts Eco-System
Sunset Beach Bridge Fails for 5 Hours
Sunset Beach Bridge Hearing Set for January 23

Taxpayer's Group Files Complaint
Push for New Bridge at Sunset Renewed After Cars are Stranded (March 1993)
Tugboat Captain is Cleared in Accident at Sunset Beach Bridge (March 1995)
Taxpayer Group Intensifies Secession Sentiment (March 1995)
Sunset Beach Needs a High-Rise Bridge
Lively Debate Expected on Sunset Beach Bridge: DOT Official Urges Courtesy
Sunset Beach Showdown: Progress vs. Quiet Haven
Modern, Two-Lane Bridge Best Option for Sunset Beach
Sunset Bridge Issue Just Keeps Going
DOT Vows to Build Sunset Beach Bridge
Clear View of Sunset Beach Bridge from Maine
Old Bridge Burdens Budget Maybe for the Last Time (March 2002)
Anti-Bridge Group Files Suit—Again
Think Before Replacing Sunset Beach Bridge
40-year-old Bridge the Only Road into and out of Town
Sunset Beach Anticipates Bridge (May 2003)

Bridge Debate Renewed (December 2003)
Judge Clears Path for New Bridge in Sunset Beach (February 2004)
Taxpayers Group Files Suit to Stop Bridge Again
The Sunset Beach Bridge Farewell to the Old, Hello to the New
Sunset Beach High-Rise Bridge Continues to Face Delays
Town to Help DOT Fight Bridge Lawsuit (October 2007)
New Sunset Bridge is not Cost-Prohibitive
Sunset Beach Bridge Snags on Suit (October 2007)
Sunset Beach Bridge Delayed: Existing Bid is Good for 60 Days (October 2007)
Property Clearing Under Way for New Sunset Beach Bridge
New Bridge Four Years From Completion

It was once said the spirit of Sunset Beach was nurtured by the isolation created by the bridge. What will the new bridge bring? The debate is finally over and only time will tell how the community will be affected by its new landmark.

The new bridge being completed with the old bridge in the foreground.

The Vesta

On April 19, 1861, six days after the surrender at Fort Sumter, President Abraham Lincoln mandated a blockade of the southern coast from South Carolina to Texas. Just eight days later, he extended the blockade to include the coasts of Virginia and North Carolina—a coastline over 3,500 miles long with many barrier islands and inlets.

For three years, the largest Federal squadron afloat was stationed at the bars on New Inlet at Fort Fisher and Old Inlet on the Cape Fear River at Smithville, now known as Southport. Their mission was to intercept specially designed steamers whose captains were determined to bring needed supplies into the Confederate port of Wilmington. At the outset, their success was spotty at best, but their odds improved with time. The Federal net caught one out of every ten runners in 1861, one out of eight in 1862, one out of four in 1863, and, eventually, every other one in 1865. When Smithville and Wilmington fell to Federal forces in 1865, severing the lifeline of the South, the end of the Confederacy was inevitable.

The story of one particular blockade runner is rife with good luck, bad luck, meritorious victory, terrible choices, and ultimately horrible defeat—all of which occurred during the same fateful night.

Before securing the anchor, Captain R.H. Eustace probably wished he had never left Bermuda. For as soon as he had, his ship, the *Vesta* was the hunted. For seven days determined Yankee cruisers chased her. She finally managed to elude them and appeared over the horizon facing the southern coast of North Carolina. Compelled to lay

to before navigating the Cape Fear River, she was spotted by a Yankee cruiser, which immediately gave chase. Soon, eleven Yankee vessels were bearing down on the newly-discovered prey. Completely surrounded, the *Vesta* turned into harm's way and ran the gauntlet in one of the most stirring scenes the war had witnessed on water. She outmaneuvered cruisers that attempted to cut her off and was so fast she was able to sprint away from the cruisers that were firing their broadsides upon her. Five cruisers gave chase firing their bow guns continually as she neared the safety of a sandbar. Despite their constant volleying, no one on board the *Vesta* was hurt. The vessel raised her flag in defiance as the shallow waters of the shoreline accepted her and distanced her from her enemy. Suffering from a single shot, which was well above the water line and had miraculously avoided flesh or machinery, victory was hers.

Unfortunately, Captain Eustace and First Officer Tickler began to celebrate their victory and it is reported that they both became outrageously drunk soon after night had fallen. It was said that the captain was asleep on the quarterdeck, stupefied with drink, when he should have put to land. At two in the morning, he woke the pilot and directed him to take the ship ashore, telling him that the ship was above Fort Fisher, when in fact, the runner was about forty miles to the south of Frying Pan Shoals. Within fifteen minutes she had run aground so hard she could not be moved.

The *Vesta* carried valuable cargo, including a grand, honorary uniform intended as a present for General Lee from some of his London admirers. Three fourths of her cargo consisted of badly needed army supplies, among them very expensive English shoes. Ironically, it had been the *Vesta's* first attempt at running the blockade.

Passengers and crew were forced into lifeboats without their baggage even though one of the passengers was a paymaster for the Confederate Navy. The final affront occurred when the inebriated captain ordered the ship fired and burned at the water's edge with everything onboard.

Yankee cruisers did not happen upon the smoldering hulk until the afternoon of the following day when the smoke from the wreck drew their attention. Nothing of any account was saved from the ship. Official records show that the

Vesta wrecked four miles south and westward of Tubbs Inlet, North Carolina, listing in just ten feet of water. She had been a fine looking, double propeller blockade runner, just like her sister, the Ceres. Brand-spanking new in late 1863, she was worth about 300,000 pounds Sterling. With her long iron hull and modern elliptical stern, she was almost 500 tons, yet barely drew eight feet of water. At 165'x23'x13', the *Vesta* was said to have been one of the finest steamers in the entire blockade running fleet.*

During the 1960s the boiler and some of the framework of the *Vesta* was visible through the decking of the pier at Sunset Beach. In fact, several slats were removed for this express purpose. The pier itself was named Vesta Pier. With time, the accreting beach covered the iron skeleton of the ill-fated blockade runner. It is now buried under the parking lot in front of the pier.

*Excerpt taken from *Shipwrecked at Sunset* by Jacqueline DeGroot

Bird Island

Although the Bird Island Preservation Society was formed in 1992, the process for securing Bird Island and deterring future development did not begin until January 9, 1996. As the last undeveloped barrier island in Brunswick County, and one of only three remaining in North Carolina, the island is truly special. Bird Island is especially treasured by naturalists including Frank Nesmith, who, through the long protection and purchase process, became an astute legal and regulatory environmentalist. His walking tours, where he physically took people to the island and pointed out the things that made Bird Island special, were instrumental in getting key players on board as many people who took his tours wrote to State and Federal officials calling for the island's preservation.

The first phase was to fight development, which many locals were able to do with the help of the North Carolina Coastal Federation, an advocacy group with employees who are litigation attorneys. But they all knew they couldn't sustain the battle indefinitely, it was costing both sides a lot of money and the ill will wasn't doing anyone any good. A ten-year battle that began in the early 90s, when the Price family announced its plans to build a bridge and causeway to the island that would serve fifteen subdivided lots and a fishing pier, had sapped everyone's energies and cash reserves. It was time to get serious and find a permanent solution; they couldn't keep doing this.

According to Camilla Herlevich, Founder and Executive Director of the North Carolina Land Trust, there are three ways to protect land and ensure it will be preserved in its natural state. One is to protest development by continually facing off against an opponent in one legal battle after another. That way had already led to a temporary standoff and it was obvious that a happy resolution was not going to be worked out between the owner and those seeking to protect the unique coastal resource that was Bird Island. Two is to buy it. At the time, the owner, the Price family of Greensboro, wanted between nine and ten million for the island. The State of North Carolina thought they might be able to come up with one million . . . maybe. The third option is for the land to be donated—that clearly was not going to happen in this case.

Buying it seemed to be the only viable option. As the environmentalists fought development and eventually stopped it, causing permits to become even harder to get and prohibitively more expensive, the owner was forced to withdraw and hold the request for permitting in abeyance. There was certainly no good will left between those who wanted to develop the island and those who wanted to preserve it. Negotiating a purchase price was not going to be easy.

The next step was to solicit help. The North Carolina Coastal Land Trust was asked to negotiate for Bird Island, and volunteers from the Bird Island Preservation Society became crucial players in the fight for the 1,200 acres of pristine beach dotted with high salt marshes, and strewn with twisted tidal creeks. With its accompanying wildlife, habitats and nesting grounds for both turtles and water birds, it is an eco-system unlike any other. Some of the plants and animals living on Bird Island would not survive anywhere else—they are too fragile. Beach-nesting birds and turtles, along with their eggs, would be prey to dogs, cats, recreational vehicles, or would simply be tromped on in a more mainstream environment. There are thirteen species of birds and animals that are rare, endangered, or deemed to be of special concern. Among the rare birds that inhabit the island are piping plovers, pelicans, wood storks, and terns. The plants tucked into the dunes are rarer still. Seabeach Amaranth, a sea grass unique to Bird Island where it manages to thrive, is so rare it's on the endangered list. Other forms of wildlife including goats, foxes, fiddler crabs, nude sunbathers, and sand crabs roam the long sandy stretches without threat of extinction. The variety of seashells boggles one's mind. But aside from the rarity of disappearing species, Bird Island, as an undeveloped barrier island, serves as protection from hurricanes. Anyone ever read John D. MacDonald's *Condominium?* (Fawcett 1985)

Then of course, there is the Kindred Spirit mailbox, home to wonderful and extraordinary stories, a place for people to record their thoughts, take solace in the tranquility, ask for spiritual assistance, and experience the landmark that has defined the heart of the community.

The special meeting on the conservation and preservation of the island was summed up with these words, "They ain't making beaches any more." The next step at the end of the regulatory battle was to develop a non-combative stance and to approach the owner of the island to determine an amount that would be considered fair for all parties. They had a willing seller and a willing buyer. And they had options to explore for securing the money.

Option three was thoroughly explored as there are tax incentives available for someone making a charitable contribution, an advantage in terms of tax credits for gifts of this nature could sometimes be negotiated if someone was able to donate part or all of the value of a gift such as this. In fact, two thirds of all land-trust land has been donated.

Once the decision was made to try to purchase, appraisals had to be done. There had to be two, both prepared by State certified appraisers. There was much information to be gathered: the exact boundaries, the wetlands involved, zoning, set backs, availability of utilities, what were other barrier islands selling for? The appraisals of $3.3 million and $3.6 million were submitted to the owner in 1997. The State offered $3.5 million.

Meanwhile applications were made for State Trust funds to secure the funding needed to close the deal. They received a grant for one million dollars. The National Heritage Trust Fund was also queried, as they were open to making some funding available to state agencies at the time. But it was all for naught. The owners thought they could develop or sell the island for more money than the land was appraised for. So the deal was off the table.

A year later the owner asked to have the appraisals updated, but North Carolina wouldn't pay to do that, so the owner agreed to pay, using one of the same companies. The new appraisal showed an increase in value—$5 million was the evaluation in 1999. The owner called Rep. David Redwine (D-Brunswick) and said this was a price he could live with. Adding that, "If you want to buy Bird Island, this is your chance." From there, Redwine set the wheels in motion. He contacted people at the Department of Natural and Environmental Resources and set up meetings with the State Property Office and with the owner. When the meetings were over, the State of North Carolina had a signed option agreement to purchase the island for $4.2 million.

Many hands worked on obtaining funding and finally some of the money was secured. The North Carolina Clean

Water Management Trust Fund contributed $1.5 million at its preliminary meeting indicating that there could possibly be more, so they became the primary source (they eventually contributed $2.8 million). The North Carolina Heritage Trust Fund offered $750,000. They had originally offered one million. The State began looking for additional Federal funding, and the Bird Island Preservation Society, sensing this was a now-or-never kind of thing, began beating the bushes. Simultaneously they applied to the State for a Stewardship Endowment. A quarter of a million dollars would be needed to provide for a summer intern and for some type of warden of the island as Sunset Beach was not going to police Bird Island—it would cost too much. Two policemen would have to be added and no revenue would be gained since the island would remain undeveloped.

Next was a series of public hearings and participation meetings where the State asked for input on planning the use of the island. Among the ideas proposed were: a summer school, a coastal nature reserve and educational outreach camp, a nature museum, an ecological research park, a tourist center with picnic tables, a pavilion for weddings, and a teaching facility. Most would have required at a minimum: bathrooms, kitchens, walkways, and handicapped access (which would have necessitated onsite parking or motorized vehicles traveling the beach). Every idea was listened to, but thankfully the environmentalists, who had fought so hard to keep development of any kind from the island, won the day. It was decided the habitat would be protected for the birds and wildlife.

The original terms specified that the owners receive all the money that year, but some of the grant money wasn't going to be available until the next calendar year so it was agreed that one portion could be purchased in the first calendar year. The ocean to the sound was bought for two million dollars in 2001. The second portion would have its closing the following year. An $800,000 charitable contribution for

Old bridge to Bird Island

tax purposes was allowed on the application. Now everyone was scrambling to find the additional money that was needed. The owners became more flexible when they realized where the money was coming from. The North Carolina Department of Transportation Enhancement Fund kicked in $700,000 as prospective replacements for sensitive areas elsewhere that would be disturbed by future road and bridge projects. NCDOT was essentially banking credits for mitigation areas—and they referred to them as Cadillac credits because the habitat was such a good one. The Bird Island Preservation Society committed to raise the money needed to establish a Stewardship Fund. The Society, in conjunction with the Coastal Reserve Program, agreed to monitor the island, manage the property, and protect the bird and turtle nesting sites.

The State acquired Bird Island from Janie Price of Greensboro in two payments that totaled $4.2 million. It was the culmination of a ten-year struggle. And the State now owns the island it had originally owned in 1823 when it transferred the title of Bird Island (100 acres at the time) to William Frink for ten dollars. Nearly 180 years later the State bought the island back (147 upland acres) for $4.2 million.

Here's something most people don't know: Tract I (1,200 acres) is owned by North Carolina, and Tract II—parts of both NC and SC—(28.88 acres) is owned by the U.S. Army Corps of Engineers.

The circus at Sunset Beach

Timeline of Events

1700 Gores settle in Little River, South Carolina.

1764 Brunswick County is carved from New Hanover and Bladen Counties—rice, tar and turpentine are major exports.

1790 Frinks, Brooks, Stanalands, and Bennetts farm 240 acres where Bonaparte and Corkins Neck are located. The area was an island.

1930s Intracoastal Waterway (1934) is developed as well as the bridge over the Calabash River. The Brooks family owned the surrounding property before the Civil War (1810-1873). Alonzo Frink owned the island and the land where Oyster Bay and Ocean Harbor are now. He sold it to Samuel Bell Stanaland who sold the island parcel to the Brooks. Brooks owned 20,000 acres.

1935 Brooks went bankrupt and sold 11,000 acres to International Paper for $8,000.

1954 Hurricane Hazel wiped out Ocean Isle. Odell Williamson and Mannon Gore ended their partnership, splitting Ocean Isle Beach and Sunset Beach with Mannon Gore getting Sunset Beach.

1955 Bald Island's name was changed to Bird Island. Gore, who had previously sold his farm in Longwood, several miles north of Sunset Beach (for $125,000), purchased four miles of land between the coast and the Intracoastal Waterway (500 acres of Gause Landing), known as Brook's Pasture. He bought ten acres of inland forest and land along the shoreline for $10,000 and $55,000 for the remainder. The first street names were recorded.

1958 Gore built the bridge and causeway to the island. By May of 1958 he had access to the island and soon had almost sixty lots ready to sell.

1959 Blane's Landing, now Twin Lakes, was platted. Route 179 was straightened.

1963 The Town of Sunset Beach was officially incorporated and the first town election and meeting were held (July 15). Eight out of thirty residents ran for office. Twenty-nine people voted. Six were elected, five commissioners and the mayor. Jobs were divided up. Mannon Gore served as the first mayor.

1964 Gore built a real estate office next to his home (where the Italian Fisherman was located). You didn't need a license to sell your own land.

1966 Tubbs inlet closed and was then reopened.

1970 The ABC store opened. Senator Roundtree from Wilmington was involved. It was a two-year project amid much controversy.

1971 A new Town Hall (dedicated to Winifred Woods, mayor) and a new Fire Department were built.

1972 A city manager was hired and the first ordinances were enacted.

1976 Land owned by International Paper became available (656 acres in the Seaside area). Ed Gore, John Williams, Paul Dennis, and Miller Pope formed Sea Trail Corporation. They built Shoreline Woods and Seaside. Mayor Kanoy and the council rejected the developments as part of the town because of the mobile homes.

1983 Larry Young began developing the Oyster Bay area, located on property leased from Sea Trail. Oyster Bay Golf Links, located on Sea Trail property, became the area's first golf course and quickly gained a reputation as one of the premier golf courses on the strand. *Golf Digest* was so impressed that the magazine named Oyster Bay "The Best New Resort Course in America."

1985 The Dan Maples Course at Sea Trail Plantation opened in October. Its overall condition quickly put it on the top of every player's "must-play list" and soon it was lauded all over the Southeast. *Golf Digest* added it to its list of the most outstanding new resort courses in the country. The Maples Clubhouse followed, offering a pro shop; The Tavern on the Tee, with fine dining overlooking the 18th green, and Brassie's Lounge. Sugar Sands and Olde Oaks were developed.

1988 Rees Jones began designing his championship golf course at Sea Trail. And, once again, *Golf Digest* chose the new course as one of the most outstanding new resort courses in America.

1989 Shortly after the Jones course opened, Willard Byrd, the celebrated architect of both the Atlanta Country Club and The Country Club of North Carolina, began work on the Byrd Course. The course begins and ends at the Jones/Byrd Clubhouse where the view from Magnolias Restaurant is simply magnificent.

1990 The Maples Swim and Tennis Club (now the Maples Activity Center) opened as a Sea Trail Plantation members-only facility.

1991 Sunset Beach and Sea Trail Plantation were named the top coastal community and "Best North Carolina Beach," by Duke University.

1992 *Money* magazine named Sunset Beach one of the best buys in the nation. *Changing Times* called Sea Trail and Sunset Beach one of the top five retirement areas in the country.

1993 The private Plantation Swim and Tennis Club at Sea Trail Plantation opened for members. It quickly became known as "The Pink Palace" because of its pastel pink stucco walls.

1996 The Chapel on the Green was completed, providing a serene place for people to pray. A beautiful brick garden honors Sea Trail residents who have passed.

1997 Sea Trail Medical Center, a joint venture between Sea Trail and Brunswick Community Hospital, opened to provide a state-of-the-art annex for the local community and visiting tourists. Sea Trail is booming, new neighborhoods providing single-family homes, town homes, and golf villas are opening all over the plantation. The Village Activity Center, which offers indoor and outdoor pools along with state-of-the-art cardio-vascular equipment, fitness classes, and children's activities opens to both residents and to the general public. After an unnamed storm it was discovered that Mad Inlet was closed.

1998- Sea Trail breaks ground for Phase I of The Village at Sunset Beach, a mixed-use development that will take ten years to complete. The 87-acre property includes shops, restaurants, offices, a pavilion, living space for assisted living, a Food Lion Superstore, and the Ingram Planetarium.

2000 In early summer, Sea Trail holds a ground-breaking ceremony for the new 30,000 square foot Carolina Conference Center. With existing facilities, there are now over 70,000 square feet of conference space making it the largest conference facility on the North Carolina Coast. *Golf Digest* in their "Places to Play" category gives all three Sea Trail golf courses a four-star rating.

2002 Bird Island is purchased by the State for $4.2 million.

2003 Sea Trail hosts the Governor's Conference on Tourism.

2005 The Fire Department gets a new building. Town Hall is renovated. The Circus comes to town!

2006 Sea Trail hosts the U.S. Open Qualifier held on the Jones Course.

2007 Magnolias Restaurant undergoes a total renovation and is renamed Magnolias Fine Food & Spirits. Sea Trail is host again to the Governor's Conference on Tourism. The First Sunset at Sunset Festival draws thousands to the beach.

2008 The Second Annual Sunset at Sunset Festival is relocated to The Village of Sunset so vendors can participate. The festival is so successful that organizers plan the event for early October every year. Work on the new bridge begins.

2010 The new bridge is dedicated. *Sunset Beach—A History* is published, authored by Jacqueline DeGroot and Miller Pope, it chronicles the history of our quaint beach town.

About the Authors

Jacqueline DeGroot and her husband Bill, bought property in Sea Trail Plantation in 1992 and began planning their early "retirement," (if one could consider it retirement with three kids in tow). In 1996 they both retired from their jobs, Jack as a general sales manager for a mega car dealership and Bill as a Fairfax County Police Detective. They built their home and moved from Northern Virginia with their son Jimmy (aged 18), son Jeff (aged 15), and daughter Kimberly (aged 10) in 1996. Jack's writing career began in Wilmington, where she spent her days after dropping her daughter off at Cape Fear Academy. Her first book was *Climax*, an erotic thriller set at Sunset Beach. It was followed by *The Secret of the Kindred Spirit*, a romantic murder mystery on the island, and *Shipwrecked at Sunset*, a fictionalized historical romance centered around *The Vesta*, a Civil War blockade runner. She had just completed *The Widows of Sea Trail* trilogy, spicy romances for the older set. She has published eleven books and co-authored three others. In 2005 Miller Pope asked for her help with *Tales of the Silver Coast, a Secret History of Brunswick County* and they have been friends ever since. You can often see them having lunch at local restaurants squabbling over issues for the next book.

Miller Pope was a partner in a New York advertising agency and a freelance illustrator. He was elected to the Society of Illustrators, a very prestigious group of talented artists. Miller and his wife, Helen, bought property at Ocean Isle Beach in 1969. They planned to build a beach house; instead that property became The Winds Resort Beach Club. For five years they spent several days out of each month at Ocean Isle Beach, flying or driving from their home in Westport, Connecticut. With each visit, it became harder and harder to leave. Both their children had left the nest, so in 1975 they moved to Ocean Isle Beach. In 1976 Miller joined Ed Gore, Paul Dennis and John Williams in founding Sea Trail Plantation. Miller's two children, Gary and Debra, now run The Winds and Gary serves on the board of Sea Trail Corporation. After a happy marriage of fifty-one years, Helen died in 2004. Miller turned to writing, largely in order to have something to illustrate. Since he had long been a history nut, and was for many years a member of the Company of Military Historians, his first effort was a history of Brunswick County, written with Jacqueline DeGroot. Miller has now written and illustrated six books and is finishing his first work of fiction.

Picture credits: Ken Buckner pages 3, 4, 5, 6, 7, 8, 12, 13, 14, 15, 43, 56, 57, 58, 86, 87, 90, 93, 96, 102, 113, 115, 126, 131. Miller Pope pages 15, 16, 17, 18, 19, 20, 21, 22, 23, 37, 41, 44, 45, 47, 48, 50, 51, 52, 53, 55, 60, 61, 62, 63, 64, 65, 66, 67, 68, 69, 70, 71, 74, 75, 76, 77, 78, 79, 82, 83, 84, 85, 88, 94, 95, 97, 100, 101, 104, 105, 106, 111, 123, 132, 133, 134, 135, 136, 137, 142, 143. Ed Gore Sr. pages 10, 11, 24, 28, 34, 35, 36, 38, 39, 124, 128, 129, 142, 143. Sylvia Henderson pages 25, 26, 27, 47, 29, 32, 47, 48. Dean Walters pages 80, 81. Sam B. Somerset page 108. Charles Lambert page 109, 138. Charles and Aileen Smith pages 116, 117, 118. Miriam Marks page 120. Dave Nelson pages 10, 30, 140. Pam Callihan pages 33, 103, 128, 129. NASA page 107. Sea Trail pages 72, 73. Seaside United Methodist Church page 110. Alex Mearnes page 141.